U0165909

全面搞定
會議英文

張其羽◎著　　會議英文的教戰手冊！

應用外語
15

ENGLISH

五南圖書出版公司 印行

筆者忝居教席近二十載，承蒙五南主編不嫌棄，獲邀撰寫此書，深感惶惑，受寵若驚。

這本小書，以會議英文為核心，蘊藏筆者英語教學與應用的個人體會，不敢名為一家之言，只是回顧過往課堂裡的種種拉拉雜雜，試圖用較為生活化、通俗化的口吻，回饋給仍在相關領域裡奮戰不懈的諸位讀友和學子，希望大家都能找到適合自己的學習方法，開竅早，基礎好，考不倒，用的妙。

筆者學養淺薄，於振筆疾書時，匆促之餘，容或造成疏漏。有任何值得參考之處，榮耀全部歸於過去教過我的恩師，以及過去被我教過的學生；有任何文字或意義舛誤，責任全由筆者一人承擔。尚祈方家先進不吝賜正。是為序。

張其羽

序言
Preface

請不妨將本書視為會議英文的教戰手冊。

第一單元幫助讀友摒除雜訊、釐清觀念，算是「飯前小菜」。

第二單元幫助讀友演練再三、熟習技巧，算是「正餐主食」。

第三單元幫助讀友挑戰自我、未雨綢繆，算是「飯後甜點」。

筆者以第二單元為本書重心，端上 15 道熱騰騰的佳餚，名之為「練習」，包含多彩多姿的情境設定。每道佳餚之後，筆者都貼心的提供了「英語文小叮嚀」與「跨文化小叮嚀」，給讀友提提味、醒醒腦。至於「THINK TWICE」一欄，同樣出自筆者拙思，相當於本書理路原料與食材配方，好奇心重的讀友可望從中獲得啟發。

如何使用本書

假如您是大專生，扣掉開學週、期中週和期末週，差不多就是一週嚐一道菜。假如您是社會人士，有工作和時間分配壓力，那麼從 15 道菜當中隨意挑幾樣嚐嚐，也頗有情趣。假如您是中學生，功課壓力頗重，那麼不妨先把菜裡面好吃的配料夾起來先嚐為快，幫自己種種英語學習的「善根」。

先賢云：開卷有益。祝大家用餐愉快！

目 錄
Contents

Part 1
第一單元

緒論 – 打破會議英文迷思

　　本書以英文簡報情境為媒介，針對會議英文場合發言的共同現象，旨在幫助在學學生和坊間各界自學，揚棄習而不察的毛病和盲點，建立可長可久的會議英文觀念和習慣。

　　首先筆者要強調的是：會議英文並非專指主持會議所使用的英文。我們十之八九，或是去當個「與會者」（聽者／觀眾），或是去當個「發表人」（講者），基本上難得有什麼機會或資格去「主持」英文會議。如果一味生搬硬套所謂的會議英文句型，就算當了主持人或引言人，那種不自然的假假，恐怕讓我們看起來更像個司儀。回想看看，過去市面上許多會議英文參考書，是不是只教我們怎麼當個彆腳的司儀，而沒有傳授我們正確使用會議英文的態度與方式？

　　換言之，會議英文可不是在叫我們事前背一大堆您想都不敢想，用也不敢用的八股文句喔！舉凡政商談判、產品推廣、心得簡報和學術會議等，皆屬會議英文範疇，其中大多數人最容易接觸到的情境，便是在英文會議當中發言。嚴格說，會議英文不一定等同簡報英文，然而簡報英文卻是會議英文的根本，要練好會議英文基本功，勢必得留意簡潔（conciseness）、具體（concreteness）和情境（context）這三項基本要求。

　　仔細推敲，我們會發現，無論是一言堂式的宣講，還是雙向互動式的詰問，都離不開一個真槍實彈的懸念：您是否經常能引發與會者的共鳴？筆者認為，所謂會議英文指的就是簡報英文在各類英文會議的情境運用。講白了，就是如何在眾目睽睽下，用英文「販賣」想法。忽略了情境因素，簡報就只是簡報，與「會議」無涉。相反的，會議英文如果只是插科打諢或行禮如儀，忽略了積極表達的

誠意和技巧，就容易淪為刻板而無趣的司儀英文或是照本宣科式的投影片朗讀比賽。

只要眾人「會而議之」，嘴裡講的，心裡想的，身體做的，都跟「英文」脫不了關係，那就是使用會議英文的時機。嘴裡講的，縱使不一定合乎文法（老外也常凸槌），但是意思總不能相差太遠，所以「選字」很重要！稀鬆平常的字眼，如果用對了，勝過十個百個費盡心思吐出來的冷僻生詞。

我們的主戰場不是在賣弄（老外眼中）本來就不怎麼樣的英文，而是透過自己已知的英文語法和文法常識，用穩健的步調和中肯的態度來呈現事實。

心裡想的，必然是當下的角色、時空和主題等情境因素，因此在參與會議之前一定要有所準備。

會前不閉門造車，會中不畏首畏尾，會後要總結經驗。

身體做的，最怕是表錯情，會錯意，所以我們必須理解（以歐美為主的）英語文化圈，到底有哪些普遍為人所接受的溝通行為模式。

您的英文再怎麼台，老外都不會怪您；可是如果

您英文很道地，裡面所反映的價值和口吻卻台到不行，那麼請別怪他們一臉茫然，甚至不想理你。

　　過去有關會議英文方面的參考書籍，有的羅列了數不清的，教條式的口袋句型，有的一味強調會議主持流程中，不同階段的串場句型。對於初學會議英文的人而言（不一定是英文初學者），如果將上述類型的參考資料奉為圭臬，真要到了開會的時候，往往一句話都派不上用場，即便勉強使出一招半式，也是詰屈聱牙，缺乏連貫性和持續力。

　　筆者並不否認傳統會議英文教材在培育英語溝通人才方面的貢獻，因為無論從什麼角度來看，從哪種路徑來學，會議英文一向有它的實用價值。有心者若願意投注心力學習會議英文，甚至只是單純記誦會議英文的制式例句，亦能夠相當程度增進英語表達能力，進而提升本身整體英文實力。

　　會議英文不見得是用來主持會議的英文，更主要是指在會議情境當中能夠製造趣味性或切身性（至少不能讓與會觀眾在心態上「棄你而去」）的英文報告。發言者愈能符合上述要求，愈能給觀眾留下深刻印象，並且在專業領域，無形中給自己加分。

　　具備公眾演說技巧，經驗豐富的發表人，自然更勝一籌；唯會議英文並不專為滔滔雄辯者所設，它更

適合於一般大眾，尤其那些從來沒有在大庭廣眾之前，眾目睽睽之下發言過的人。

即便會議英文有它的專業性，然而這類情境更容許發表人在一定限度之內的「不完美」。例如：發表人可能口條欠佳，可能用字不妥，可能緊張忘詞，可能重複囉嗦，可能聲音太小，可能過於激動，可能速度偏快，可能目光單一，可能時間被摳，可能簡報故障，可能擋住視線等等，不一而足，而我們就在這樣的不完美基礎之上，先求有，再求好。說穿了，

　　會議英文發言本身就是一門尋求回饋的表演藝術。

　　既是粉墨登場，就不能太單調，也不宜太過火。行禮如儀，照本宣科，只會讓自己和與會觀眾漸行漸遠；刻意的語不驚人死不休，同樣能讓觀眾吃不消。唯時代在變，步伐在變，觀念在變，會議英文閱聽的習性也在改變。《孫子兵法》有云：「知己知彼，百戰不殆。」我們會議英文情境當中的潛在觀眾，拜聲光科技和網路技術之賜，隱然具有下列傾向：一是*缺乏耐性*，這意味講者需要適度剪裁所使用的語句，且內容不宜過度冗長；二是*容易分心*，這意味講者需要掌握節奏，適時拋出與主題相應的觀念或試問；三是*好簡畏繁*，這意味講者需要簡化看似複雜

的事實與數據，必要時，以圖代文；四是*喜新厭舊*，這意味講者必須不落俗套，至少要能「用不同方式表達同樣意思」。

Part 2
第二單元　抓住會前演練要領

練習01（任務目標：釐清報告來龍去脈）

常聽到這類勵志假說：「如果你的生命只剩下X天，你打算怎麼過這最後的日子。」即便是最渾渾噩噩的人，陷入了上述命題困境，也會抖擻起來，想想在人生的最後幾天要做什麼（what to do），怎麼去做（how to do it），以及為什麼要這樣做（why）。筆者並非刻意賣弄黑色幽默，因為極端的條件有時能幫助我們更瞭解自己；所以當我們準備會議英文簡報時，同樣一句話就變成了：「如果只給你三分鐘時間發表，你打算怎麼辦？」在如此苛刻的前提下，我們別無選擇，只能去蕪存菁，優先而且擇要地談三件事：動機（why），方法或流程（how），以及成果與結論（what）。因此本練習重在「知己」。

作業想定

找一個日常生活中你最熟悉的話題，將它開展成一份英文口頭報告，但是你只能用不到三分鐘的時間，向假想中的與會觀眾簡略說明簡報內容。在這之前，你必須打個草稿，幫助自己釐清想法。

Step 1 粗擬初稿

Topic> Doing Housework Makes Me Manage Time Well

Why> I'd like to live a dfficient life / I find my friends share the housework live a better life

How I do it when I work long / I do it while I am working / I do it while learning

What It helps me relax / It helps me work and earn a lot more

　　以上框框內的文字只是前置作業而已，暫時先別考慮用字或文法，只要擠出點子就可以。如果實在沒有想法，當然只好到網路上找靈感。但其實想到什麼寫什麼比較要緊，千萬別扼殺了自己的創意。在思維上，先把自己逼到牆角，然後丟出想法，接著再用下一個想法銜接下一個想法，只要抓住想法和想法中間的基本邏輯和因果即可。無論您是否有足夠的生活或工作經驗，想法不是光靠死背或抄襲就有的，而是要養成延伸式的思考和表達習慣。

Step 2 審視初稿

Topic Doing Housework Makes Me Manage Time Well

Why I'd like to live a dfficient life / I find my friend share the housework live a better life

How I do it when I work long / I do it while I am working / I do it while learning

What It helps me relax / It helps me work and earn a lot more

　　劃底線者：拼字錯誤，用字籠統

劃雙底線者：時態不對，句型欠佳

劃波浪線者：用字累贅

劃粗底線者：時間不明

劃點狀線者：點子離題

Step 3 修改初稿

Topic> Doing Housework Makes Me Manage Time Well

Why> I'd like to live an efficient life / I found my friend who shared the housework made the most of their time

How> I do it after I work long / I do it while working / I do it while learning

What> It helps me relax / It helps me work smart

　　前置作業完成後，接下來想想看，上場後要說些什麼。初稿是只是把原先瑣碎的想法，串連成前後呼應的句子。但是如果要延展成為三到五分鐘的口頭說明，恐怕還是力有未逮。首先必須定義何謂有效率（efficient），一旦下了定義，就必須保持一致，往後的口語表達內容完全依照這個定義來走。

　　比如說，如果您將「效率」定義為「又快又好」，那麼下面所舉的例證，就得符合這個定義，否則便有可能離題或不知所云。由於就像發現到有些有做家事的朋友，往

往是愈忙愈能善用時間，因此讓您起了見賢思齊的念頭。至於要如何達到目標，就看您的時間是否分配得宜。本來做家事是件吃力不討好的事，但是因為受到了朋友的啟發，您的重點會是：一，利用工作之餘來做家事（其效果是調節身心)；二，利用工作之際來做家事（其效果是節省時間）；利用學習之際來做家事（其效果也是節省時間）。

　　依照上述方法套招，逐漸地，以做家事為媒介，把事情做得「又快又好」，您不只節省了許多時間，而且能夠調整身心。結論雖說不上另類，卻足以引發並保持聽者的興趣。

Step 4 撰寫講稿

　　有了初稿，再來就是把它開展成為一篇口頭論述。在撰寫講稿的時候，應儘量動筆，腦子想到什麼，就寫什麼，彷彿自己已經佇立在講台上，面對著眾多與會者的目光。講稿寫來不是要讓您背的，而是要幫助您模擬講台上的情境，瞭解自己能說什麼。就像寫作文那樣，等過一陣子再看，您會發現哪些不足，哪些可刪，自然會再修修改改。

Hello everyone, I am XXX, a student at YYY university. When I was a boy, I was very slow in everything. People always say time is money. I know, but I just couldn't make it. Time management is a popular idea. I didn't know

how important it is until my college roommate, a young man from Seattle, also a friend of mine, helped change my mind and told me what to do. Here, today I am sharing you with my experience about how I changed from a slow man into a fast man.

上面這段「起手式」，裡面大有玄機。因為我們在〔練習2〕還會詳加探討，所以這裡只是簡單交代一下。目前您只需記住，在這個階段，要努力把「人」和「事」串連在一起。在會議英文的場合，一般來說，「起手式」最容易擄獲人心，卻也最容易失去人心。您不必故弄玄虛，但也不應該過於呆板。觀眾想聽的，您可以猶抱琵琶半遮面，適度吊一下胃口，他／她們最後會感激您。接下來的步驟，是要擴充既有的草稿，以供口語表達之需。

解釋 Why I'd like to live an efficient life
善用 Because 或 It is because

Because I was too slow in everything, I paid a lot of price. For example, I was often late getting up, late taking school bus, late coming to class, late for exams, and late for dates. At school I got low grades; although I studied hard, being late makes me absent from many lessons. Finally I got flunked because I went for exams late and so

was rejected to take them. What's worse, after class, I always kept my girlfriend waiting so long. She dumped me. All these make me regret, and I wanted to change for the better, for a more efficient life.

以上是交代緣起，就是解釋動作慢吞吞給您帶來的種種的苦果，讓您發憤後下定決心有所改變。然後話鋒轉到室友給您的靈感。

重點 what to do / how to do it
技巧 narrative（像說故事一般）

My roommate Jason is an American. In the beginning, I supposed he wouldn't do any household chores but focused on his lessons. But I was wrong. I found he put everything in good order. He did the laundry himself. He swept the floors inside and around our dormitory. I thought he must have been very busy. What surprises me much more is that he is a top student who often gets straight A's. Of course I shared housework with him. The thing is that I did it slowly and I took it as a duty.

One day, Jason reminded me, "Are you all right? You look unhappy every time you did housework." I said,

"No, I didn't. I was just worried about how much time I could spend on my lessons after finishing housework." He replied, "I guess you probably did the wrong way at the wrong time." Then he suggested that I choose to do it when I feel tired after studying for a long time. I tried, and it worked! Jason also suggested that I memorize new vocabulary, for example, when sweeping floors, washing clothes, cleaning the house, etc. To be honest, at first I didn't get used to it. However, people say, "Practice makes perfect." The more I did it that way, the less time I spent. I mean, if I take my school lessons and housework as a batch of tasks.

　　大體上，您已將口頭英文內容的主體部分交代完畢，現在輪到下結論了。初學者下結論的時往往不知所措，多半把先前提過的東西簡略地炒一次冷飯就結束了。這樣雖然也是無可厚非，但是總讓人覺得好像少了點什麼。筆者建議，如果實在不曉得說什麼才好，不如就談談主題對您的意義或影響吧！

　　Now I understand time is precious. Doing many things at the same time seems not a good idea for those who are used to doing one thing at a time, but it really makes me pay more attention to what I am doing. Besides, doing housework is not necessarily a hardship. That depends on

how you are thinking about it. Studying lessons and doing housework support each other. I see both as a role-play game, which is very fun and makes me relaxed somehow.

Step 5 編寫簡報

可優先考慮放入投影片的關鍵詞，名詞有：efficiency 效率、time management 時間管理、doing housework 做家事；動詞片語有：live an efficient life 過有效率的生活、manage time 管理時間、do/share the housework 做／分擔家事、work smart 巧為，和work hard 力為（和「巧為」形成對照）。

THINK TWICE

Whenever you have to orally present something within a limited period of time, the three points that are most attractive to your audience may include

(1) what causes or motivates you to choose the topic;

(2) what methods you apply or/and what stages you go through; and

(3) what you have achieved and found.

As to point 1, it sounds irresponsible to say "I present this just because I feel interested in the topic." Fine. Then what? Such an answer will never satisfy the audience. If possible, they will question you, "why do you feel interested in it?" The question usually refers to what others have done about the topic, such as the existing theories, viewpoints, findings, etc., which makes you believe that there must be something more you can add to it.

In regard to point 2, general statements like "I did a lot of experiments" or "there are many stages through which the results are rendered" appear unclear and thus fail to satisfy the audience. You'd better mention the key terms, at least, which best describe the essence of the methods used, such as "my electronic survey collects responses primarily from the adults over 30 years old," "I attempt to justify my hypothesis through the questionnaire results," or the like. Speaking of the stages or processes, you will find it efficient to focus on the most decisive or

most difficult stage or process.

Point 3 could turn out boring and meaningless if it looks textually familiar to the audience. Instead of repeating what has been presented, you need to interpret the results and, if necessary, share certain implications based on them. Although the ways to conclude a presentation may vary, it is a must for the presenter to make sure whether the findings correspond to what is claimed or assumed in the beginning.

When you try to make a presentation very briefly like that, you will have to quickly decide how much time should be spent on each point. The safest way is to spend equal time on each point. If you are going to highlight whichever point you think worth more notice, surely you will stay much longer with it. However, the situation is that you are only given a short period to finish everything, so in practice the price you will have to pay could be too high because the rest of the points would be crowded out if you insist on lingering.

英語文小叮嚀

這裡所謂書面簡報，指的是您上台報告時用的投影片（slides）。一般會議英文的場合，上台發表報告，常見發表人一個勁兒的讀著投影片裡的文字，幾乎一字不漏，從頭念到尾，一張接著一張，錯把投影片當成了口語簡報的救命仙丹，唸完後，下台一鞠躬。這是筆者所見過最糟糕的簡報模式之一，在學校課堂、學術研討會和商務會議裡，如此照本宣科的情形，卻是屢見不鮮。

要知道，投影片最主要的功能，對講者來說，是「備忘」（reminder），對聽者來說，則是「提示」(cue)。設計簡報投影片，固然重在吸睛，卻也不能將所有要講的話，鉅細靡遺、一字不漏地放到投影片裡。上乘的簡報投影片內容，字數愈少愈好：能用句子，就不要用段落；能用片語，就不要用句子；能用單字，就不要用片語；能用圖示，就不要用文字。一旦確立下來，則最好保持一致（consistency）。

照著投影片所列的內容念，雖然不能證明您是否具有會議口語表達能力，但是至少已經表明了您沒有表達的誠意。與會觀眾會覺得：既然如此，乾脆發給我一份copy還來得快些，我好歹自己在家看，不必專程跑來現場聽著別人照唸。一個發表人的專業性和自信心，靠那幾張投影片，唬得了一時，頂不了整場。到了問答階段（Q & A session），一兩個問題接不上招，還是會被搞得灰頭土臉。

　　會議英文最大的特點，即是口語要鬆，書面要緊。鬆的意思是，儘管您英文再好，不必刻意賣弄艱澀的詞藻，反倒應該多多使用簡單句型，最多搭配一個次要（從屬）或對等子句，一句一句，娓娓道來。投影片內容如果使用文字，則應力求簡潔明晰，行有餘力，再考慮押韻和雙關等修辭技巧。

跨文化小叮嚀

　　包括台灣人在內的東亞人士往往不習慣眼睛直勾勾地看著他人。對歐美人士而言，直視對方，恰恰能展現自己的誠意和專注。東西方會有這樣的差異，其背後原因相當複雜，不在本書探討的範圍。無論如何，當您有機會上台發表英文簡報，即便帶著一口破英文，只要能和現場觀眾保持一定的目光交流，總比自顧自的獨白，正眼也不瞧觀眾一下，要來得令人印象深刻。

　　筆者建議，在正式上場發表之前，不妨給自己做一番心理建設：「台下觀眾都是我的靠山。」或者：「為了答謝與會觀眾的聆聽，我一定得跟他／她們保持充分的眼神交流。」不過要留意的是，眼睛不應該只是注視會場裡某位來賓，以免讓人感到緊張。比較適切而不失禮的竅門是，用掃射的方式來分享您的目光。

　　分享目光時，頭頸轉動可以慢一些，眼球倒也不必真的投注到任何一位嘉賓身上，而是心裡大致將觀眾席區

分為四塊。換言之，觀眾再多，對您來說，充其量只有四位。等到時間久了，上手了，不怯場了，就可以逐步增加心中設定的觀眾區塊，最終養成平均掃視的習慣。

練習02（任務目標：不著痕跡誘發共鳴）

台灣流行過一陣子「帶動唱」，它和有氧舞蹈感覺很像。參加有氧舞蹈，多半有志一同；參加「帶動唱」，則為情勢所逼。每當台上有人發難，大搞「帶動唱」，台下的熱絡，總是難掩一絲尷尬。會議英文的場子亦然，如果發表人一開始即不斷發問，咄咄逼人，或是像站野台、打選戰那樣地大聲吆喝，美其名是誘使觀眾投入，其實往往搞得大家不知如何是好。講者理當不卑不亢，身先士卒，做好暖身，也幫觀眾暖暖身：或從自己的體驗說起，或透過日常生活的例證使在場觀眾瞭解講題的普遍性，最好能讓聽者產生切身的感受。如果能夠把聽者的興致帶動起來，剩下的事就好辦了。

作業想定

找一個日常生活中的熟悉話題，假定未來要將它開展成一份英文口頭報告，現在先針對這份英文口頭報告試擬一段開場白。開場白口吻要像講故事那樣，帶出主題的普遍性和切身性，旨在引發共鳴。

Step 1 粗擬初稿〈正例〉

Topic > Does Recycling Work To Trash Reduction?

〔版本一　**Yes, it does.**〕

Good afternoon. When I just came here, in this room I found no trash. You know I came from a college where

classrooms are always full of garbage, such as waste papers, dumped bottles, spilled coffee and food scraps. We hate garbage, but we cannot stop increasing it. In that sense, there is no choice but doing our best to recycle the trash we produced.

參考詞

waste papers（廢紙）
dumped bottles（棄置的瓶子）
food scraps（廚餘；殘羹剩菜）
recycle（資源回收）

上述例子所使用的策略四平八穩：先分享切身體驗／經驗，顯露出問題本身的普遍性，然後提出矛盾難解之處，據此大略揭示解決問題之道。才短短不到一分鐘，您就跟觀眾拉近了距離，同時表明了自己解題的立場。只是千萬要留意：「起手」階段，用字不宜艱澀，但應該適度放入若干關鍵詞，將聽者帶入主題情境之中。不過，如果細究本例遣詞用字，恐怕虛線的部份會有點偏題，而且可能讓在場或不在場的相關人等感到不快。比較安全的表達方式是對事不對人，或者避免指明特定對象。因此不妨改為正面表述，將原稿修訂如下。

Good afternoon. Now I feel cozy, not simply because

of your hospitality, but the room where we are now is very clean. You know we teachers sometimes are annoyed by a classroom where there is a lot of trash, such as waste papers, dumped bottles, spilled coffee and food scraps. We hate garbage, but we cannot stop increasing it. In that sense, there is no choice but doing our best to recycle the trash we produced.

　　修改後，雙底線的文字雖然是場面話，但是顯得比較平易近人，而且避免了不必要（且可能造成離題的）的批評。與會觀眾如果大多有教師身份，想必對於這段開場白心有戚戚焉。

Step 2 開展初稿（正例）

　　Good afternoon. Thanks for giving me the opportunity to share with you my findings on this topic. [pause（停頓）] I like here. Well, it's not just because of your hospitality, but also the room where we are now is very clean. You know I've been teaching in college for years. We teachers sometimes feel annoyed by a classroom where there is a lot of trash, such as waste papers, dumped bottles, spilled coffee and food scraps. My students feel the same, but for certain reasons we just cannot help producing trash. [pause] What I am trying to say is, we hate garbage, but we can-

not stop increasing it. In that sense, although not all trash is recyclable, there is no choice but doing our best to recycle the trash we produced. If well disposed, some trash can be transformed into reusable stuff like fuel, manure, reprocessed paper, and so on.

　　只要時間允許，沒有偏離題旨，會議英文的口語，原則上不嫌囉嗦，尤其開場的時候，無論用字、句型還是文法，儘量簡單明瞭。涉及主題的關鍵詞，亦不嫌重複。臨場若不確定該用什麼連結詞（或不想濫用連結詞），可適度用停頓來替代；停頓有時設定用來期待觀眾回應的笑聲（如範例中第二次停頓）。

Step 3 粗擬初稿〈反例〉

Topic ⟩ Does Recycling Work To Trash Reduction?

〔版本二　**No, it doesn't.**〕

　　We *are living* in the world where the number of population and that of trash production are in direct proportion. We'*ve had* a strong belief that recycling helps to reduce trash, but the statistics and data I've collected, as I am going to show you today, will prove what we have firmly held untrue. Recycling does not reduce trash but simply slow down the garbage production. In the long term, we *will all be swamped* in garbage.

　　上述寫法，直接點出癥結，帶出問題的普遍性：人口增長，製造的垃圾也多。資源回收再利用，只是減緩垃圾增長速度，長遠來看，無法徹底減少垃圾製造量。整體而言，修辭略嫌正式，無可厚非，結尾則亦莊亦諧，語出驚人，誘發觀眾進一步聆聽的興趣。代名詞we本身不能保證產生「親和力」，但由於後續所銜接的一系列動作，如are living, 've had (a strong belief), will all be swamped等，方才塑造了「感同身受」的效果。

the number of（…的數量／數目）
prove ... untrue（證明…為不實）
slow down（減緩／慢）
in the long term（長遠來看）

　　或者可以換一種方式切入，從切身經驗開始，逐漸導向問題的普遍性：

　　When I studied in college, my economics professor told us, "If you want to make something small, *tax it*!" I am not sure if my professor was right. But as a citizen in Taipei, I am pretty sure when I *was requested to* pay for littering, I started to pay more attention to recycling and became more aware of how much trash I could produce every

day. To save money, I've chosen to *litter* less, like most of my neighbors. So is recycling a good idea to reduce trash? Well, it is not until people have to *pay the price for* littering.

　　像這樣故事性很強的開場白，最容易引人入勝。故事內容當然是事前經由一番構思所得，甚至不排除找親朋好友幫忙做個彩排。此外，這個例子並不全面推翻論題，而是有條件反駁正方看法。至於應該採取哪一種論證手法，依然要看您手上掌握了多少資料，以及整體報告的一貫想法和立場來決定。

參考詞

tax it（抽…的稅）
be requested to（被要求去〔做〕…）
litter（丟垃圾）
pay the price for（為…付出代價）

Step 4-1 開展初稿（反例之一）

　　Where there is humankind, there is garbage, and vice versa. [pause] Actually garbage was not a problem until the Industrial Revolution, and the problem got worse after the 1950s, when mass production became popular in manu-

facturing. [pause] We've had a strong belief that recycling helps to reduce trash, but the statistics and data I've collected, as I am going to show you today, will prove what we have firmly held untrue. If we notice how much progress humans have made in the past two centuries, we'll see that mass production of goods always ends up with mass production of garbage. [pause] As to the garbage produced, some are recyclable, but more are irreversibly useless. That's why recycling does not reduce trash but simply slow down the garbage production rate. In the long term, we will all be swamped in garbage. [pause] Our hope for environmental protection should be based on alternative methods and necessary innovations to be applied in all industries.

　　展開後的版本所使用的策略，在用字和文法方面，由簡入繁；在說理和論證方面，由因推果。新版捨棄了開頭正經八百的片語（in direct proportion「成正比」），改用大家較為常用的，且經過講者改編的俗諺模式。中間四次停頓，是為了幫聽者爭取消化反思的時間。

Step 4-2 開展初稿（反例之二）

　　When I studied in college, my economics professor told us, "If you want to make something small, tax it!" Many years later, after moving to Taipei, I found I

had to pay whenever I littered. I started to pay more attention to recycling and became more aware of how much trash I could produce every day. My professor is right. At least I know I wouldn't care that much about recycling if I were free from any "garbage tax" [using hand signals（兩手的食指與中指同時伸出，快速微彎一兩下即可，彷彿兩對兔子耳朵在向人打招呼）]. I once chatted with my neighbors; they told me they tended to litter less simply because doing so would save money, although they never deny that recycling is a good idea to help protect our environment. [pause（停頓）] I've chosen to litter less, like most of my neighbors. So is recycling really a good idea to reduce trash? It could be great, but I will cast a doubt on that if governmental policies fail to create incentives.

　　此一版本的策略是「說故事」，從講者個人經驗出發，經驗中隱藏了題旨的核心論點，逐步帶入正題。講者並不直接反駁資源回收或再生資源對垃圾減量的貢獻，而是漸次鋪陳，指陳政府政策所提供的誘因才是解決問題的關鍵。由於只是開場，所以此處並不需要急於提出詳細的數據或重要佐證。用字方面大致淺顯，只有最後一字 incentives（誘因／激勵）或許對在場英文底子較弱的人來說有些吃力，不過因為報告內容的重點無非圍繞在這個

字，因此聽者只需經由上下文意，加上講者稍後的深入解析，便可分曉。

THINK TWICE

It is much easier to attract the audience at the beginning of a conference talk. Even so, when the presenter stands onstage, there must be something needed to bridge indifference and unfamiliarity. Down there the viewers may anticipate what is to be performed soon, but the fact is that a lot of them are not exactly interested in the chosen topic and could choose to be absent. They show up to observe the talk for varied reasons. That's why the presenter needs to do what seems interesting to them.

First of all, we should be very clear about how people usually define the so-called "interest", which is often synonymized as "fun". Being fun is not easy, while different members of the audience are dissimilar in feeling fun. Interest, rather, is more like a factor aimed at concern or curiosity. If one feels concerned or curious about

something, definitely "that thing" is of interest to him/her. Since "it takes all sorts to make a world," a presenter should figure out what could be the common denominator believed to effectively arouse the audience's concern and curiosity.

When dealing with "concern", the presenter can consider a person, issue, time, venue, or/ and object that has been often discussed or debated recently. For example, if "climate change" is the topic, you can start with, in a warm-up manner, a story about a well-known meteorologist assuming global warming, about the places where weather abnormalities prove most destructive to their ecological environments, about when the Kyoto Protocol was signed and came into effect, etc.

When narrating the warm-up story in the beginning, the presenter is expected to create certain "tension" or "conflict" to help the audience's curiosity persist. For example, according to the

topic chosen above, first, the opposite ideas against global warming can also be introduced to draw further attention; second, how residents who live in the devastated places have struggled and what they have achieved; and the cacophonies found among the states which agree upon the Kyoto Protocol.

Once the audience get mesmorized, gradually, by such an "onstage rehearsal", they are more likely to become attentive and proactive. In short, because the audience simply need a reason to care, a presenter who rarely bothers to meet the need will find it more difficult to win the audience's heart back if the post-introduction sessions turn out dull or chaotic.

英語文小叮嚀

因為英語不是我們的母語，所以使用起來難免力不從心或辭不達意。在會議英文的場子，某些初學者為引起觀眾注意，會用一些聽起來很艱澀的字眼，或者用一些聽起來語氣很強硬的動詞，如此一來，往往達不到應有的效果。

　　開場如果非得使用難字或罕字不可（尤其與報告主題直接相關的專有名詞），則必須略加說明之，否則聽者若是感到一頭霧水，跟不上後來的簡報內容，甚至失去了繼續聆聽的興趣，最後倒楣的還是我們發言者。因此，最好改用較為淺顯易懂的詞彙，直到簡報中後段再適時、適量且逐次加入難字。

　　一般來說，開頭不需要刻意展現武斷，畢竟決勝點是在接下來的論理和佐證說明。初學者英文力道拿捏不準，有時開場用字過強，會讓聽者感到不舒服。想要化解這樣的窘境，不妨多多利用副詞、情態助動詞和從屬子句；當用字過輕時，它們就會是您的油門，當用字過猛時，它們就會是您的煞車。本書稍後筆者會另闢練習專章，供讀友們再三揣摩。

跨文化小叮嚀

　　以英語為母語的外籍人士傾向獨立思考和相互辯證，不喜歡說教，更不樂於聽他人說教。說教即是從上而下的單向灌輸，和長期受個人主義薰陶的文化格格不入。除非旨在互動參與或問答研討，一般會議英文的簡報宣講過程不見得總能夠做到雙向溝通，因此講者多半會自覺或不自覺地運用口頭和肢體語言技巧，來拉近自己和觀眾之間的心理距離。開場階段更是如此，以吸引目光，贏得好感為優先。

　　例如：登場後並不直接進入正題，而是稍微花一點

時間，故作輕鬆，語氣隨和，彷彿和熟識者閒聊似的，或交代緣起，或攀親帶故，或來段故事（涉及主題但不著痕跡），或自我解嘲，或和主持人／引言人（如果有類似的人物在現場的話）插科打諢一下；非口語層面，或來回走動，或走近觀眾，秉持動作穩健，眼光平均分散給觀眾的原則。

　　參與英文會議，身為講者，如果您歷來的習慣是打從一開始上台就「躲」在講桌或電腦操控台後面，眼光永遠「落」在投影布幕或眼前的電腦畫面，嘴巴老是照著PPT裡的東西在唸，那麼請您不妨換位思考一下：假想自己坐在台下聆聽，站在您前面的講者總是「躲」在講桌後面，眼光永遠「落」在投影布幕畫面，嘴巴老是在「唸」PPT，那會是什麼樣的感受？

　　換言之，一開場，無須先聲奪人，但務必「走出去」和「說出來」，把自己逼到火線上，才是最安全，最能跟觀眾站在一條陣線的做法。

練習03（任務目標：掌握措詞力道輕重）

　　筆者曾自告奮勇，在沒有任何外來資源挹注的條件下，牛刀小試「翻轉教室」，當一名獨行踽踽的磨課師（MOOCs）。即便「縱橫」講壇多年，教過來自五大洲的學生，但叫我當著機器鏡頭（其實只是一台iPad）自顧自的說話，錄製課前教學影片，還是感到十分困窘。幸好一回生，二回熟。從此我堅信，矗立在面前的鏡頭，不是一台機器，而是一個活生生的聽者。這種觀想的好處在於，用「一對一」的口吻發言，語氣不至於過重，因為「見面三分情」，說話通常會留一點餘地。慢慢的，在錄製過程中，自己意識到：副詞、情態助動詞和副詞子句，原來這麼好用。

作業想定之一

　　試擬九個英文句子，前面三個表達情感／情緒，中間三個表達意見／立場，後面三個表達願望和訴求。初稿用較強烈口吻，修訂稿則試著分別運用副詞、情態助動詞和副詞子句，把口吻調整得比較圓緩或委婉一些。

Step 1 粗擬初稿

I don't like the way she talks.
They were in a bad mood.
The poor hate the rich.
We see eye to eye on that matter.
I do not agree with you.

Democracy is a necessary evil.

We chose to continue corporal punishment.

There is no way out but taking my proposal into account.

Study hard!

Step 2 修改初稿（加了副詞之後）

By and large, I don't like the way she talks.

They were in a bad mood **sometimes**.

The poor **seemingly** hate the rich.

We **finally** see eye to eye on that matter.

I do not agree with you, **honestly**.

In a sense, democracy is a necessary evil.

We chose to continue corporal punishment **despite its controversies**.

Unavoidably there is no way out but taking my proposal into account.

Under such circumstances, study hard!

　　副詞可以是一個單字，可以是兩個字以上的詞組。此外，我們也不能忽視「介系詞 + 名詞」的組合。「介系詞 + 名詞」按所在位置判斷，有時產生形容詞的作用，有時則產生副詞的作用。

修改初稿（加了情態助動詞之後）

I **wouldn't** like the way she talks.

They **must have been** in a bad mood.

The poor **could** hate the rich.

We **will** see eye to eye on that matter.

I **would** not agree with you.

Democracy **must be** a necessary evil.

We **would** choose to continue corporal punishment.

There is no way out but **having to take** my proposal into account.

You **should** study hard! (或者You **had better** study hard!)

情態助動詞有一個字的，也有兩個字的（如had better, have to等）。情態助動詞如果涉及現在，後面接原形動詞；如果涉及過去，後面接動詞的完成式。最後一例為了加入情態助動詞，只好把隱藏在使役語氣背後的You搬出來用。

Step 4 修改初稿（加了副詞子句之後）

I don't like the way she talks **whenever something makes her proud**.

When it ended up with failure, they were in a bad mood.

The poor, **if they feel economically exploited,** hate the rich.

We see eye to eye on that matter **although it was not easy to negotiate**.

No matter how much effort we've made, I do not agree with you.

Democracy is a necessary evil **because nothing is perfect**.

We chose to continue corporal punishment **simply because parents wanted it**.

Provided that there is no way out, my proposal **will** be taken into account.

If you try to survive, study hard!

相較之下，副詞子句能幫助講者擴充概念，解釋想法，在口語方面顯得游刃有餘。特別要提一下：倒數第二例的provided that意義近似於if，但是比if的因果條件限制更加嚴格。換言之，如果一定要有A，才能有B，那麼A的前面就用provided that。

作業想定之二

從日常生活中選材，擇定一個爭議話題，據此發表簡報，長約三分鐘左右。在作簡報之前，先擬定英文草稿，運用副詞、情態助動詞和副詞子句，把口吻調整得比較圓

緩、中立或委婉一些再上場。

初稿參考

Topic> Is Abortion Amoral or Immoral?

When we hear the word **homicide**, at the first moment we <u>probably</u> won't tell how terrible it means. If we choose to say killing or murder, we <u>will be very likely to</u> feel negative about them. Abortion, like homicide, is a euphemistic expression, but it is even more indirect. It comes from abort, a verb that explains an action to fail, cease, end, or stop at an early **stage**. When we add "i", "o", "n" to it, the meaning changes into **pregnancy termination**, which equals killing a baby inside, <u>although the baby is still an embryo or fetus</u>.

To talk about whether abortion is amoral or immoral, we need to define what abortion is and what it may mean to the whole society. However, first we need to reach an agreement about our general understanding of morality. How would you define it? [暫停，凝視觀眾，並稍待片刻] To make it short, morality means certain principles that tell us what is right. If we are doing the right things or doing things in the right way, we are moral. For example, in my country, **yielding seats** to **senior citizens** is something moral. When people choose not to do it, we will say they

are immoral, but obviously they are not guilty. <u>If they don't accept such a moral</u>, yielding seats must have nothing to do with morality. For them, it is amoral. Whether yielding seats or not, <u>physically speaking</u>, no one gets hurt.

So, abortion seems immoral. Killing babies inside is some sort of homicide. But if people argue that **embryo**s are not lives, abortion <u>would</u> become amoral. We just cannot ignore the fact that the way we define "life" is quite **arbitrary**. Suppose there were germs **fossil**s found on **the Mars**, scientists <u>would</u> say, "Wow, once there were lives on the Mars. <u>If a germ is a life</u>, there is no reason to deny a human embryo as a life. To make things clear, we <u>should</u> not cheat ourselves like that any longer.

What about a **fetus**? Isn't it a life? It <u>might</u> not be appropriate to suppose that a human fetus is not a life just because of its **immaturity**. <u>Supposedly</u> fetuses are unable to see or hear; that should not be taken as a **convincing argument** that helps explain they are lifeless. <u>If the argument makes sense</u>, then the **debate** over **mercy killing** and those **vegetables** lying in bed for years <u>would</u> appear **absurd**. Likewise, seeing fetuses as **lifeless** is arbitrary.

We got to understand that abortion is unusual, <u>although today it is more often performed</u>. We also need to be aware of what seems **universal** from the past to the

present, and even to the future; that is, homicide is immoral [pause]. In that sense, abortion **in essence** is immoral <u>although sometimes it could become amoral</u>. When **address**ing the **issue** of abortion, we <u>should</u> be honest and responsible. We need to admit that abortion is **exceptional**. It has to be performed due to **force majeure** or something <u>morally</u> **excusable**.

並非所有的副詞（包括副詞子句）和情態助動詞都是用來表達委婉語或中立語氣；這要由上下文意來決定。如果多少涉及委婉或圓緩之說明作用，則用底線標示以供讀友參考。生字和關鍵詞另以粗體標示，供讀友自行查對。

THINK TWICE

Suppose most of our audience at an English conference are English natives, surely they will not be afraid of direct confrontation in most cases if the debate is based on facts, data, and reasoning. However, even though there were no confrontation intended but words or phrases inappropriately expressed, the audience might feel offended or confused.

Before you get onstage to give a talk or make a presentation in public, you'd better look up in the dictionaries the key terms and the difficult vocabulary. Sometimes Chinese-English dictionaries exist as a dangerous lure to the Chinese-speaking presenters who will have to talk at an English conference. Without bilingual reference, the terms or vocabulary could be misunderstood and misused. However, it takes time to comprehend the vocabulary entries in a bilingual dictionary, let alone those in an English-English dictionary. One of the most frequently used tactics is to use familiar words or phrases, not necessarily general ones, while using another familiar word (usually adverb or adjective) or a familiar clause to modify or elaborate them.

For example, an expression like "although the results do not exactly correspond to what was assumed, such implications as follows are expected to provide inspiration to whoever is interested in related studies in the future" could be unfamiliar to a beginner whose mother

tongue is not English, who possibly would rather say, "although the results are different from my assumption, we can still learn some lessons." The problems are that the term "results" in itself is different from "my assumption" because an assumption is not a result, and that the term "lessons" is too general/vague to explain how important they seem . A modified version the beginner could take into account is like "although the results are different from the *expected* results, we can still learn some *meaningful* lessons," or "although the results *unexpectedly* (or *surprisingly*) *differ* from my idea, they could be *very meaningful*."

In the conference situation, a presenter's good command of what has already been acquired matters much more than how difficult the words or how complex the sentences he/she will be able to use. The case is simply like the poor people without enough money, so their attempt to make the most of the money they have had is quite understandable. The bottom line is that

your expression should be made as faithful as possible to what you really think to avoid unnecessary offense or misinterpretation.

英語文小叮嚀

　　副詞、情態助動詞和從屬子句只是配套工具，有其特定作用，不是目的。假使您用字恰如其份，那麼完全可以不必考慮使用上述工具。況且要強化或弱化發言語氣，也不是非副詞、情態助動詞和從屬子句不可。

　　用字不妥或力道拿捏不準，隨著閱讀經驗的增長和認字能力的提高，問題會逐漸獲得改善。讀友如果想徹底提升英文兩大表達能力－說和寫－勢必得多多接觸英文報刊雜誌，熟習從屬子句用法。從屬子句包括三大類：名詞子句、形容詞子句（或稱為關係子句）和副詞子句。子句玩熟了，英文才算是學通了。

　　如果下定決心打好英文句型基礎，市面上參考書好用的還不少。筆者受惠最多的，中英對照版有旋元佑先生的系列專著，英文版有Betty Azar的文法系列教材；諸位讀友即使站在書店裡翻它幾頁，也會深感獲益良多。

　　我們常認為西方人（尤其美國人）講話或論理喜歡開門見山，這種看法大致不錯，可是莫將「開門見山」誤解為「亮出底線」或「攤牌」。這種西方式的開門見山，多半出於起承轉合的需要，意在提綱挈領，以便聽者掌握大要或理解講者基調，真正的好戲其實在後頭；如果沒有經過講者的層層論辯或雙方的對話激盪，最好避免先入為主。

　　老派的英國人傾向推砌大量詞藻，高度重視修辭，哇拉哇拉攪和了半天，加上迥異於美式英語的「正統」腔，常令老台摸不著邊。相較之下，老美表達方式淺顯、通俗而平易近人，容易給東方人「打開天窗說亮話」的印象。美國人雖然沒有英國佬那般囉嗦，卻也有他／她們自己的一套婉語模式（euphemism），就像語言馬賽克那樣，在表達自我的同時，不至於觸怒他人。

　　整體而言，如果不是出於心理疾病或個人教養問題，以英語為母語的西方人士說起話來，大致有禮有節，層次分明，遇到有爭議的話題，除非必要，話不會說得太直白，但最低限度能夠讓人體會到他／她們的立場或基本觀點。如果修辭不慎，用字過猛，語氣偏強，就會顯得唐突（offensive）沒禮貌，給人留下壞印象。筆者以為，和老美打交道，凡事據「理」，則「力爭」必然獲得同情；遇事講不出道理來，一味力爭，那就是「無理取鬧」，對方決不吃這套。

練習04（任務目標：理順發音咬字難處）

筆者初出道時，曾四處兼課，主授英語聽講練習。一天，筆者和學生們討論《101忠狗》劇情，要求所有人必須輪流登台用英語發表一分鐘心得。輪到一位帥哥，講不到幾句，總在那裡「屌沒遜、屌沒遜」個不停；我心生疑惑，特地請他暫停，解釋啥叫屌沒遜。因為我模仿他的屌字發音特傳神，旁邊某好心同學小聲提醒道：「老師，他說的是Dalmatians，大麥町狗啦！」剎時，全班哄堂大笑。在全球化當道的時代，英語發音固然有腔調之別，即便「隨和風趣」和「專業嚴謹」是會議英文的兩大法寶，假使講者發音咬字始終離離落落，那麼恐怕擁有再好的法寶，也使不上力。

作業想定之一

從右至左，由上而下，反覆朗誦下列字群。子音收尾正確時，會和後字起首母音之間產生漂亮連音。發長母音時，嘴唇緊張；發短母音時，嘴唇放鬆。發 [ʌ] 音時，假裝把輕音 [ə] 發的重一些，勿念成 [ɑ] 音。

a cup   a cu**p o**f coffee   a cu**p o**f coffee costs less

〈發音須知〉正常速度下，a, u, o皆唸 [ə]，力度上，一輕一重一輕，因為中間是所謂的倒V音 [ʌ]。cost還好，但costs就有違中文發音習慣，我們最好小心因應，老老實實給它連發兩個無聲子音 s 和 ts（有如中文「斯

刺」，但是喉嚨不振動；如果出了聲，喉嚨一定振動，那就錯了）。

two cups　two cup**s of** drinks　two cup**s of** drinks cost much

〈發音須知〉正常速度下，cups的u和of的o皆唸 [ə]，力度上，一重一輕。drinks尾巴有s的無聲子音，請務必老老實實地發出來（有如中文「克斯」，但是喉嚨不振動）。

a bunch　a bun**ch of** flowers　a bun**ch of** flower**s** **o**n the desk

〈發音須知〉正常速度下，a, u, 以及of的o皆唸 [ə]，力度上，一輕一重一輕。flowers尾巴的s唸 [z]，屬有聲子音，唸的時候如果喉嚨有振動，那就對了。假使貪圖便利，沒有確實收尾，或是收尾收得不正確，flowers on二字的發音就會變成 flower-on或flower-sson；一旦中間的s-on [zɑn] 音發不出來，或者發成無聲子音的s，那麼這段詞組的連音就算是失敗了。聽者的注意力往往一而再，再而三的被這類連音「失聯」（通常講者會重複犯同樣毛病，很少有例外）的意外所阻卻，這對講者來說，很不划算。

ma**ke up**　ma**ke u**p for　ma**ke u**p fo**r a** lack **of a**bility

〈發音須知〉正常速度下，make和up串在一起的發音，聽起來像是may-cup。再者，for和a最容易被忽略，事實上這兩者之間還是有連音的。按美式英語發音，for的r需要稍微捲舌，於是兩字串連就成了fo-ra。接下來，lack of ability三字以中間的ck-of-a發音最為緊要，只要字字收尾確實，串起來的發音聽起來就像 [kəvə]。我們無須為連音而連音，只要發音收尾做的好，連音自然就會冒出來。

take　take par**t in**　take part **in u**nofficial **a**ssemblies

〈發音須知〉part和in串在一起的發音，聽起來會是par-tin。緊接著in後面有un的字首母音，串連收尾後，聽起來就是tin-nun。最後，unofficial的尾音l需要令舌尖抵到上面牙齦，於是和後面assemblies的a之間就拉出一個漂亮的 [lə] 音。

a sto**ne**　a sto**ne i**n the pocket　a sto**ne i**n the pock-et **ow**ned by him

〈發音須知〉stone尾巴的n音，必須令舌尖抵住上牙齦，和in串在一起的發音，聽起來就是nin。當然了，in尾巴的n，同樣需要令舌尖抵住上牙齦。而pocket的t如果有收尾，和後面的own串連後聽起來就像是tone。

the storm　the stor**m is o**ver　storms　storm**s are o**ver

〈發音須知〉storm這個字發音結束時，因為有m音，所以嘴巴應該是閉上的。如果不閉唇，就無法與後字is的i產生連音。隨後的over和is之間也會出現連音，不過需要留意的是，is的s唸 [z]，屬有聲子音。旁例的storms發音結束時，先短暫閉唇，再發 [z] 音，以便和後面的are形成連音。至於are和over之間的連音，不必刻意，只需特別專注於are字的收尾，一定要有r音才行。

word　utte**r a** word　utte**r a** word **a**nd **a**sk for it

〈發音須知〉word的or在英文屬超級捲舌音，而utter的r只需稍微捲舌即可。從word開始到ask結束是最具發音挑戰性的部份，建議從後面往前練：先唸ask，然後and ask，然後word and ask，就會感覺比較簡單而自然。

world　wonderful world　wha**t a** wonderful world

〈發音須知〉world切不可讀成word，中間的r和l，一個捲舌，一個抵舌，轉折務必清楚。

the Mill　the Mil**l** **o**n the Floss　the Mil**l** **o**n the Flos**s** **is a** novel

〈發音須知〉mill須收尾，和後面的on串連後，聽起來會像m-ill-lon。floss尾巴無聲，is尾巴有聲，和a串連後，聽起來成為 [flossi-zə]。

note　no**te** **a** novel　not**e** **a** nove**l o**f the noble

〈發音須知〉這裡無論el或le，尾音全發l，舌尖必須上抵。抵舌的l音和長母音O是兩個完全不同的發音，切勿混淆使用。

religion　the origi**n** **o**f the religion　the origi**n** **o**f the religio**n** **i**n that region

〈發音須知〉粗體黑字已標示連音位置，這裡不再贅述。不過必須提醒一下，例中origin，religion和region三個字的g都是發成 [dʒ] 的音，唸的時候，可以噘嘴，但不可嘟嘴，否則就變成了像中文「居」字的音，那樣聽起來就很怪了。通常把G唸成「居」的人，往往在另三個發音

位置近似的[tʃ]、[ʒ]和 [ʃ]，也會犯同樣的嘟嘴毛病；最好能一併改正。

　　experience　experien**ce an e**xperiment　experien**ce an e**xperimenta**l e**rror

〈發音須知〉昔日台灣某政要在美國發表公開演講，雖然本土腔調很重，但是大致能讓人聽懂，獨獨有一個字的發音，用了幾次，全部唸錯。那個字就是惡名昭彰的experience。別說是外語能力極佳人士，我們一般初學者，恐怕大多沒能把那個字讀對。但其實有解藥的。請記得把它拆解成ex, pe, rience這三個部份來唸，保證日後一定不會再讀錯。其中ex唸[ɪks]，pe唸 [pɪ]（p在s之後，實際要唸為b音），而rience唸 [rɪəns]。

　　knoc**k o**n the door　knock**s o**n the door　knock**ed o**n the door

〈發音須知〉單複數或時態所導致的連音問題，亦應獲得同等重視。第一組由原形動詞起首，接on，所以連音是 [kan]。第二組動詞由於受潛在第三人稱主詞影響，動詞以s收尾，和on之間形成 [ksan] 的連音。第三組則使用過去時態，動詞末尾有ed，接下來連音就成了 [ktan]（按發音常識，ck屬無聲子音，緊接在後的ed就跟著無

聲，所以唸 [t] 不唸 [d]）。

　　運用前述發音咬字觀念，將練習3的例文重唸兩次，中間念錯也別在意，念的時候要一氣呵成，可以慢一點，但是儘量不要中斷。文中粗體字是需要留意收尾和連音的部份。中間遇標點而隔開的前後兩字之間，代表語氣停頓，不可連音。後面遇連接詞，或表示列舉，或表示銜接了從屬子句，雖無標點，卻有語氣停頓的需要，同樣不宜連音。

　　When we hear the word homicide, at the first moment we probably won't tell how terrib**le i**t means. If we choose to say killing or murder, we will be very likely to feel negati**ve a**bout them. Abortion, like homicide, i**s a** euphemisti**c e**xpression, bu**t it is e**ven mo**re i**ndirect. It comes fro**m a**bort, a verb tha**t e**xplain**s an a**ction to fail, cease, end, or sto**p at an ear**ly stage. When we add "i", "o", "n" to it, the meaning change**s i**nto pregnancy termination, which equals killing a baby inside, although the baby is sti**ll an e**mbryo or fetus.

　　To tal**k a**bout whethe**r a**bortio**n is a**moral o**r i**mmoral, we need to define wha**t a**bortio**n i**s and what it may mean to the whole society. However, first we need to rea**ch an**

agreement about our general understanding of morality. How would you define it? To make it short, morality means certain principles that tell us what is right. If we are doing the right things or doing things in the right way, we are moral. For example, in my country, yielding seats to senior citizens is something moral. When people choose not to do it, we will say they are immoral, but obviously they are not guilty. If they don't accept such a moral, yielding seats must have nothing to do with morality. For them, it is amoral. Whether yielding seats or not, physically speaking, no one gets hurt.

So, abortion seems immoral. Killing babies inside is some sort of homicide. But if people argue that embryos are not lives, abortion would become amoral. We just cannot ignore the fact that the way we define "life" is quite arbitrary. Suppose there were germs fossils found on the Mars, scientists would say, "Wow, once there were lives on the Mars. If a germ is a life, there is no reason to deny a human embryo as a life. To make things clear, we should not cheat ourselves like that any longer.

What about a fetus? Isn't it a life? It might not be appropriate to suppose that a human fetus is not a life just because of its immaturity. Supposedly fetuses are unable to see or hear; that should not be taken as a convincing argument that help**s e**xplain they are lifeless. If the argument makes sense, then the deba**te o**ver mercy killing and those vegetables lying in bed for years woul**d a**ppea**r a**bsurd. Likewise, seeing fetuse**s a**s lifeles**s is a**rbitrary.

We got to understand tha**t a**bortio**n is u**nusual, although today i**t i**s mo**re o**ften performed. We also need to be awa**re o**f what seems universal from the past to the present, an**d e**ven to the future; tha**t i**s, homici**de is i**mmoral. In that sense, abortio**n i**n essen**ce is i**mmoral although sometime**s i**t could beco**me a**moral. Whe**n a**ddressing the issue o**f a**bortion, we should be honest and responsible. We need to admit tha**t a**bortio**n is e**xceptional. It has to be performed due to force majeure or something morally excusable.

做完練習之後，或許日後對待連音這回事，就不會那麼便宜行事或掉以輕心。可千萬不要以為到時候上了場，非得這樣唸不可喔！實際發表的時候，絕不能像機器人那樣，完全沒有超出規劃以外的停頓；有時講者感覺需強調某字，或感覺某字發音掌握的不是很流利時，或只是單純為了引起聽者注意，當然需要略作停頓。但凡是因為臨場需要所做出的任何停頓，並不需要，也不應該刻意為了連音而連音。筆者重申：連音是正確發音收尾的自然結果，不是目的。

會議英文講者最好在正式上場發表之前，確實彙整自

己可能用到的生字或難字，尤其對於那些可能令聽者感到陌生的專有名詞，以及有別於母語發音習慣的單字和長串詞組長連音，務須反覆演練；遇發音不熟之處，務必查證清楚，甚至向同行英文能力佳者請教。

上場後，如果依然對生字和難字發音沒什麼把握，不妨考慮用其他較為平易的單字或詞組來表達相似概念（但是在簡報投影畫面中仍應該保留原用詞彙），或者每當唸到發音不順的單字或詞組，試著放慢速度，不必急。我們有多少實力，就用多少速度去表達。口語表達這種事，先求有，再求好。講者的目標是要讓觀眾聽得懂，跟得上。

THINK TWICE

If you know how to listen, you will know how to speak. The statement is pretty much like that between how to read and how to write. It explains the core nature of the input-output relationship in language acquisition. However, listening carefully is not a guarantee of correct pronunciation. If one chooses to ignore the sound that was supposed to be uttered on an ending letter, he/she will be always misunderstood. And it has not much to do with one's accent.

Taiwanese students, for instance, despite being familiar with numerous vernacular ending sounds, which are hardly pronounced in Chinese Mandarin, appear careless about the ending sounds in English. Sometimes they are confused between [O] and [l], such as the two separately ending in *radio* and *racial*. More problems are found in consonants, whether silent or sounded. It is easy to be aware that many Taiwanese tend to read storm as *storng*, grown as *grong*, coward as *kaor*, triumph as *try-um*, find as *fine*, and so on. Such a phenomenon is not so much a misreading as a bad habit.

Haste makes waste. It makes no sense that a passenger will choose to get off the bus right before its upcoming arrival at the stop just because he/she is so hurried. Likewise, whatever pronunciation characterized by neglecting its ending sound will be regarded as incomplete and thus fails to facilitate effective communication.

　　英腔和美腔何者較優，至今沒有定論。留美的，講的英文自然是美腔；留英的，往往流露的是英腔。何況土生土長的澳洲人和歐洲人，自然也有其澳腔和歐腔。所謂腔調（accent），指的是長期以來，後天習得的，自覺或不自覺的發音習慣。即便同一國族內部，也有各自不同的腔調，因此實在不必把腔調的差異看得太嚴重。

　　可是話又說回來，在學習英文的過程中，每當遇到了發音障礙，或者因為鄉音難改，或者因為外語繞口，反正打死不願正音，明明一直唸錯，卻屢屢推說是自己的「腔調」使然，固執如是，久而久之，一定會對自己的英文口語競爭力造成負面的影響。腔調差異是一回事，發音錯誤是另一回事，一碼歸一碼，不宜混為一談。

　　腔調差異主要體現在母音的發音歧異，聽起來好像是發錯了音，卻「錯」的頗為一致，而且明顯受到了母語發音習慣的影響。發音錯誤則主要體現在三種現象，要不就是同一個母音發音錯誤且不一致，要不就是母音和母音之間張冠李戴，要不就是子音收尾不確實，不到位，以至於和後續單字的開頭母音失聯，無法產生正確的連音，常使聽者感到迷惑不解。

　　現在學英文比以前方便的多，照理說並不存在查字典費時耗力的問題。琳瑯滿目的線上免費字典任君挑選，還附帶真人發音（不是那種死板板的電腦合成音），只需動

動手指，多聽兩遍，多練幾次，發音障礙自然排除，勤能補拙。

　　和美國人談天有個好處，就是您如果錯字連篇，對方仍展現風度，耐心傾聽之餘，三五時會重複一下您剛剛難得講對的字，表示同意或讚許，並搭配一個帶有鼓勵意味的堅定眼神。假如對方不完全同意您的看法，那麼在回應時，會換一個字，甚至換一種講法，來詮釋您剛剛的意思。久而久之，兩人之間的交情漸漸升溫，您的英文口語也大有進步。

　　話題，習慣上從不痛不癢的事情開始，或是從跟彼此本身沒有直接關聯的事物談起（天氣、交通、流行音樂、運動賽事等），慢慢切入到工作、生活、感想和經驗分享，然後視情況，如果談得投機，自然能愈聊愈深。或許將來有一天，話閘子打開了，還能聊到藝術、哲學及其他知識性和專業較強的話題，讓人家對咱們刮目相看，自己的口語自信心也更加提高。所以說為什麼我們平常一有空就應該練練功，探探對方文化的底，讀讀英文報紙，看看英語新聞，起碼要知道人家現在流行什麼，關心什麼，順便把日常生活的好用、常用詞彙記一記，否則「書到用時方恨少」，明明滿腔熱誠想要海聊一番，卻是「話到嘴邊留半句」，豈不可惜也哉？

　　但是也有不少讀友感到挫折，尤其當我們和老美聊的

正愉快，一下子腦筋轉不過來，詞窮，對方立刻就把話接了過去。這下可好，從此換對方講個不停。其實不是不讓我們講，而是老美的口語表達習性，很少有「留白」的空間。對她／他們來說，溝通主要靠嘴巴說出來的文字（拼字文字的起源和特色不正是如此嗎？），留白等同於溝通停頓，容易造成尷尬。

下次遇到這種狀況，無需氣餒。大不了轉換一下角色，讓對方去侃，您就專心傾聽，遇到精彩或令人不解的用字，不妨跟對方坦誠表達您的讚賞或疑惑。老外也是人，跟我們一樣，心思敏感細膩的很，可別白白把對方當成練習英文口語的「沙包」，那樣就不太有禮貌了。

練習05（任務目標：揣摩簡報備忘竅門）

在筆者學生時代，上台報告使用電腦投影的情形並不普遍。剛開始，PPT風格傾向簡樸，聊備一格。當時英文會議講者的成敗，主要取決於口條。口語不行，或者準備不周，只好死心塌地的念稿。不過短短數年，PPT到處都有，人人會做，簡報投影以爭奇鬥豔為能事；逐漸地，臨場照本宣科者眾，面眾侃侃而談者寡。直到前些時候親睹台大葉丙成教授蒞校發表心得報告的風采，這才印證了筆者多年潛藏在心底的秘密：原來，會議報告備忘的最高境界，不在於製作精美的投影片，而在於用最簡省的書面內容，達到最大的備忘效果。觀眾千里迢迢跑來參加英文會議，不就是要聽我們講者「現」身「說」法的嗎？

作業想定之一

針對某時事話題，以英文完整句型，選定立場，提出三個基本論點（做為日後開展口頭報告的藍本）。其次，將這三個英文句子簡化為三則英文片語（使其不存在「主詞＋動詞」的結構），但是每則片語的詞性和字數必須保持一致。然後依序按照「字母排序」、「字首聯想」和「接龍推論」等方式，修改這三則片語，使其將來適用於投影片，以資備忘。

Step 1 粗擬草稿

Topic ▷ Should the Ministry of Education Take Measures to Close Colleges Just Because of Their Low

Enrollment Rate?

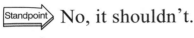

Standpoint No, it shouldn't.

Arguments

1. The market decides what colleges will survive because it is a matter of **supply and demand**, so the M.O.E. needs to do nothing but let go.

2. For **the rule of law**, no government agencies or departments should force, whether directly or indirectly, any lawfully operated colleges to close down.

3. Taking measures to close colleges violates **policy consistency**, for it is the M.O.E. that welcomed more schools to get promoted to colleges.

　　從草稿中擷取主要論點的關鍵詞（粗體字標示）之後，就可以開始進下一步。在簡化的過程中，冠詞可以先去掉。

Step 2 粗擬草稿簡化草稿

　　若按字首「字母排序」，假定下列是一張投影片，它的內容就會像這樣：

policy consistency

rule of law

supply and demand

可是因為這三則片語的字數並不一致，詞性雖然都是名詞，形式上卻不盡相同，所以仍需要稍作修改。經過一番量身訂做，兼顧字母排序，重整之後，可以轉化為：

版本一　　rule of consistency
　　　　　rule of law
　　　　　rule of market

版本二　　consistent policy
　　　　　due process
　　　　　free market

版本一的rule of二字明顯重複，既屬累贅，不如盡刪，只保留consistency, law, 和market這三個字。版本二則試圖用「意譯方式來呈現關鍵詞，如果講究一點，還可把音節不一致的consistent policy改成音節數目和另外兩則片語接近的agreed program。

若按「字首聯想」方式（acronym）排列，舊版本policy consistency, rule of law, supply and demand（PRS），版本一（CLM），以及版本二（CDF或ADF），都找不到任何可以提供聯想的諧音。如此一來，就得另起爐灶，從草稿論點的字裡行間尋找線索，進一步

061

推敲文意，轉化表達形式。經過一番努力，不只可以鍛鍊英文敏感度，同時有助於增進瞭解自己所要發表的內容。以下是可能的一種呈現結果：

market
agreement
democracy

這三個單字雖然不一致，音節卻漸增（2，3，4），也算是有某種題規律。起首字母（MAD）有生氣或瘋狂之意，便於聯想和記憶。

若按「接龍推論」方式排列，就不必刻意考慮字母排序或字首諧音的問題，而是儘可能使得上則片語（或單字）的末尾字母和下則片語（或單字）的起首字首相同，以便產生有如接龍般的音響效果，同樣有利於聯想和記憶。

long-term business
supply and demand
due process of law

接龍方式無法面面俱到。雖然三則片語的屬性都是名詞，但是長的樣子都不一樣：第一則的名詞主力在最後一字，由前面的long-term來修飾；第二則的兩個名詞由

and作媒串連：第三則的名詞主力在第二字process，分別由前面的due和後面的law來修飾。這個例子的賣點除了接龍本身，還有相同的音節數目；光看它們所製造出來的音響效果，就足以讓聽者擊節歡賞了。

作業想定之二

　　針對原稿，寫一段英文短句，將來要做為投影片的首頁。它可以是不痛不癢的開場白（以離題為準），也可以是一段發人深省的引句或雋語。然後，請發揮巧思，在這段英文當中「暗藏密碼」，讓自己可以在不看稿子，另外增加投影片頁數的情況下，以口頭說明本題的三個基本論點。

草稿參考

　　"Don't tell **pe**op**le** how to do things, tell them what to do and let them **surprise** you with their **r**esults."

　　　　　　　　　　　　　　-- George Patton, U.S. General

　　前面這段文字要放在投影片裡，差不多就是在標題頁之後，然後講者口頭上可以表達如下（即將呈現出來的，就是一副能夠侃侃而談的架勢）：

　　To describe the problem we face today, I would like to quote what Charles Dickens wrote, "It was the best of

times; it was the worst of times." The good news is, we've had a lot of colleges and universities, more than needed. If we have enough money, enough time, and strong will, then go ahead please. The doors are open. The thing is, when it matters not much to us because there are too many open doors, then why do we have to keep them? For those who work and live on these doors, that could be a bad news. An idea that could be taken into account by the government is to dismantle some doors of our higher education system. Maybe we can take it more seriously to have more doors closed, not to simply have more doors smashed. So, my points are, first, taking measures to close colleges will violate policy consistency, for it is the M.O.E. that welcomed more schools to appear as or get promoted to colleges or universities; second, the market decides what colleges or universities will survive because it is a matter of supply and demand, so the M.O.E. needs to do nothing but let go; and thirdly, due to the rule of law, no government agencies or departments should have any lawfully operated colleges close down.

　　密碼就藏在投影片引句的粗體字標示，像是people裡的p和l就是policy consistency的密碼，surprise有supply的部份諧音，而results裡的r和l就是rule of law的隱語。

　　筆者以為，密碼就是密碼，所以粗體標示純粹是為了方便讀友參考。臨到上場時，暗藏密碼的投影片，文字內容還是以清一色為好。不過，自認記性較弱的講者，或可採用色系相近的顏色來標示，這樣比較不會引起觀眾側目，像是這樣：

"Don't tell people how to do things, tell them what to do and let them surprise you with their results."

-- George Patton, U.S. General

THINK TWICE

　　Presentation is an art affected by the interplay between the speech/lecture performer and the conference audience with the fact that the former is expected to play a dominant role. However, the number of conference presenters is larger than imagined who overtly change their presentation into either a slide show demonstration or a reading activity. That appears like a countercurrent which traces back to the "good old time" when there were no such gadgets as computer, WWW, PPT, and even slide projector.

What has gone wrong with conference presentations is that many presenters, especially non-native English speakers, do not bother to "express" themselves. They simply read out what they have prepared. A relatively shorter period, if any, is given to the end of the presentation – Q&A session, where the audience will have the only chance to observe how the presenter argues for his/her own stuff in a substantial manner. In a sense, the countercurrent is the same as wasting everybody's time because the supposed presenters have become slide readers, who obviously digress from what a conference presentation may mean.

Therefore, those who are willing to speak out in public and take action accordingly are potentially qualified for the position of a conference presenter. As for a presenter, sticking to the slide show mode or the "live" reading mode is neither a guilt nor a shame. It is, to be specific, a loss of opportunity not merely of proving oneself able to think and speak English but also

of building up the strengthin one's own English expression.

　　書面簡報PPT的作用除了備忘，就是引導。為了能讓觀眾留下深刻印象，簡報投影片裡的內容最好以精簡為要，如果能夠帶進一些音節或諧音等方面的規律性，那麼必然有利於講者的聯想和鋪陳，同時更有利於聽者的理解和記憶。

　　就像音樂的不同調子能誘發諸如喜悅、激昂和悲傷等感受，英文的格律（meters）也能製造類似效果。例如，大部份英文詩詞自然流露著抑揚格（iambus）的韻采，而揚抑格（trochee）則特別用在氣勢磅礴的講詞，其單字重音經常先強後弱，給人激昂雄渾的感受。以行文口說步調而言，長母音比短母音，或是拼字較長的單字比拼字較短的單字，更能給人步調趨緩的覺受。

　　英文和中文最大的差異，在於前者是拼音文字，後者是表意文字。拼音文字在圖象上能夠發揮的空間有限，所以非常重視音效，這在口語表達方面特別明顯。英語世界裡主要的新聞頭條，或是官網發佈消息，為了吸引讀者目光，挑起興味，常會製造一語雙關（偶爾玩過火了，也造成非議，像上回Linsanity正風行，體育記者一句chink in the armor便引起興論譁然），或者狂押頭韻（字首採相同字

母，如wanderers wasted water in the west）。

提到雙關語，我們不能不想到「用典」的問題。典故並非洪水猛獸，只是客觀工具。濫用之，令人生厭；善用之，勝過千軍萬馬。英語世界裡，典故的主要來源有三：一是《聖經》文學，二是《希臘羅馬話神話》，三是可供相互參證的早期文脈。前兩項答案明顯，重要性突出，自不待言；第三項則需稍作說明，例如談到NBA、MLB，用典常涉及過去明星球員和經典賽事。老外的典故，我們自然不是那麼熟悉，只好多看，多讀，多聽，多查。

跨文化小叮嚀

西方人習慣線性思維，口語表達彷彿吃飯喝水，信手拈來毫不費力；東方人縱使拙於言辭，由於巨大的文化習性差異，總無法像前者那般「巧言令色」，因此在建構文字方面可以算的上是強項。可惜的是，會議英文的決勝點並不在文字建構，而在口語表達。報告是否能令觀眾久久回味不已，主要取決於下列三種因素。一、觀點新穎；二、層次分明；三、表達流暢。我們的文字功夫再好，總得把它恰當的講出來，附帶必要的口頭說明和分析，才有臨場的意義。

前兩項因素，對於勤勞好學的東方人來說，通常不是問題。但是想要表達流暢，就不是那麼簡單的一回事了。筆者過去有些來自歐洲的外國學生，自恃英文能力很好，從頭到尾連珠炮似的講了一大堆，前後邏輯連貫，層次分

明，但是細察其實質內容，基本上空洞無物。若干從小生長在美國的ABC也有類似毛病（我在擔任研究所入學口試委員時遇過幾回）。令人不禁感慨：口說能力強，不等於會議英文能力高，更不表示學養能力在水準之上。

既然如此，我們與其對簡報投影檔案產生莫可名狀的心理依賴，誤認投入大量時間準備投影片，就是在準備會議英文了，還不如仔細地想想，怎樣才算是言之有物，又怎樣才能讓我們所準備投影素材產生最大的備忘效果，要來得牢靠許多。

練習06（任務目標：控制口語速度節拍）

　　筆者念國一時，班上來了位短期遊學生，有香港背景。印象最深刻的兩件事，一是在同學們請求下，他教會了我們如何罵三字經；二是在英文口頭即席報告時，他用那沒有句讀（逗），風馳電掣般的英語，一口氣講了五分鐘，把大夥唬的一愣一愣，下台前贏得如雷掌聲。坦白說，我們一句都沒聽懂，也沒興趣知道他說了什麼。在那個社會相對閉塞的年代，他簡直就是大家心目中的神。多年後，筆者念了博士，為做研究，打越洋電話向美方洽購資料，哪曉得接話的老美，講話之快，令人窒息；昔日港仔同窗的口語速度，恐怕只能算小兒科。午夜夢迴，不禁反思：別說是英語了，講話有必要講得這麼急嗎？

作業想定之一

　　從報章雜誌中任選一篇英文評論，讀三遍。第一遍請細讀，用筆圈出自己認為值得特別強調，尤其與題旨息息相關，或與主要論點契合的詞彙。第二遍就照自己平常一般的速度去唸，但遇到剛剛圈起來的關鍵詞彙時，必須稍微放慢速度。第三遍請重複第二遍的動作，假想自己面前有一群觀眾，當唸到關鍵詞彙時，除了稍微放慢速度之外，可抬頭往前，假裝大略掃視眼前並不存在的觀眾。

範文參考（改編自筆者 2003 年 8 月 28 日發表於 *Taipei Times* 的評論）

Topic Reading Is the Key to Improving English

The authorities concerned will adopt a new English curriculum for senior-high school students. According to the curriculum, the students will have to acquire at least 7,000 vocabulary entries. They are expected to be **equipped** with the ability to listen, speak, read and write to an **acceptable** degree before graduation as well. Then what? Can this measure be regarded as a **guarantee** of high proficiency in English among these **quasi**-undergraduates?

Students on average nowadays are getting slightly better at listening and speaking, while they are obviously weaker in reading comprehension. What seems **frustrating** is that many of them cannot even make up a full sentence. Such a **phenomenon** leaves much room for discussion. However, it is worth more attention that "the inability to read and write" is the same as "illiteracy", despite the fact that English education for the youth in Taiwan has achieved great success in upgrading vocal and aural skills.

Will memorizing more vocabulary prove helpful to bridge the gap between "illiteracy" and "literacy"? Well, that sounds **ambiguous**. According to Dr. Darrel Doty, "It seems easier to express yourself by using complex words,

but how well you master a language depends on whether you can apply easy words you've learned to (complex thinking)."

"Make your writing as readable as possible," said another English professor, "Simple words and simple sentences are quite **desirable**." It seems one's English (proficiency) has been mistakenly (judged) and (assessed) by touchstones like an (extensive vocabulary).

When local students, especially older ones, start to learn English, they must find it extremely (difficult to think) in the language. This is a crucial problem that may decide the way one will be dealing with the language, and it is also a difficulty supposed to be overcome first. Make much effort to get used to English syntax and feel (comfortable) with the use of it; otherwise the more words one memorizes, the more **frustrated** one will become.

If one's vocabulary is limited, **definitely** one won't be able to express oneself easily. However, even if one's vocabulary is large enough, how (adept) is one at using it? Or even though one has a small vocabulary, does one care for (making the best of it)? What's more, does one read (often)?

Experienced English learners may question the arguments above and say: "How will one be able to read without the required or basic vocabulary entries?" Well, the same question could be asked this way: "Although one has mastered a large amount of words, does that assure one's ability to read?" A lazy high-school student who is doomed to failure is very likely to consider the new **threshold** set -- 7,000 vocabulary entries memorized -- a "mission impossible" because he/she doesn't bother to read.

If one rarely reads, how possible is it that one's word bank will be **enriched** with a better vocabulary? If a person's vocabulary is limited, how can he/she feel motivated to read? Diligent students, however, are believed to read regularly; thus acquiring 7,000 words is probably a piece of cake for them.

How much one has read and understood serves as an **indispensable** factor that motivates one to keep learning English. Therefore, in terms of English proficiency, reading-oriented programs will sound more valid to help train and evaluate young students than the number of words acquired does.

　　本例中圈起來的部份，屬論點重要詞彙，應適時放慢速度（或唸的時候加重一點力道）；粗體字屬生、難字發音，也是應該放慢速度，讓講者有時間發好音，咬好字，使聽者有機會聽得懂，跟的上。

　　本文開頭（第一個段落）第三個字concerned後面的ed發音最容易為人所忽略。這裡的ed雖屬有聲子音，實際的發音操作卻是「無聲勝有聲」，只需要把捲曲完畢，正要回歸原處的舌尖，順勢抵到上牙齦偏內側的地方（之後立刻彈開），喉嚨甚至都還來不及振動出聲，就算是完成了正確的發音收尾了！第三個段落倒數第三行末尾的learned字，其ed收尾也有異曲同工之妙。

　　第二個段落倒數第一行前端有個achieved，尾巴ed的發音操作也頗有「無聲勝有聲」的味道，差別在於，這整個單字的收尾要先從上牙輕觸下唇內側開始，完成後，才順勢將舌尖抵到上牙齦內側（之後立刻彈開）。倒數第二個段落的倒數第三行，believed這個字的收尾也相同之妙。

　　倒數第三個段落中，第四行的asked，同樣必須收尾，只是這個單字雖短，發音卻不是我們（以中文為母語的人士）所習慣的那樣。它只在發出了第一個聲音a（音標 [æ]）之後，後面就統統「熄火」，連續跑出三個無聲子音 [s] [k] [t]。讀的時候，這三個無聲子音一個都不能少，否則收尾就不正確。

 作業想定之二

　　從報章雜誌任選一篇英文評論，讀三遍，不必瞭解文意。讀第一遍的時候，慢慢唸，順便標示出（自認）發音不易的生、難字；全文唸完後，上網確認這些詞彙的正確發音。讀第二遍的時候，照自己平常一般的速度去唸，遇到生、難字（已知何正確發音）時，請務必放慢速度，咬字清楚。讀第三遍的時候，每當快要接近劃了底線的字之前，請停頓半秒。

範文參考（引自筆者 2005 年 9 月發表於 *Asian ESP Journal* 的論文摘要部份）

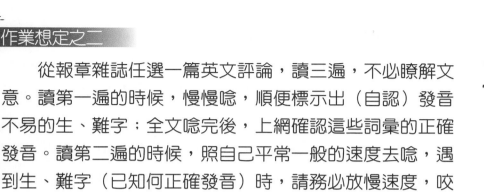

Topic ⟩ How American Culture Correlates the Process of Globalization

　　It is arguable <u>that</u> every culture may be deemed a **potential** but imperfect model <u>that</u> other cultures can **consult**. Although many regard it as an incarnation of democracy and a **crystallized** or **epitomized** model of human civilization, the United States as a cultural entity is definitely an imperfect one, which does not necessarily "direct" the process of **globalization** to the right track. As such, what this paper mainly concerns includes, first, why America has long been considered an easy target criticized as cultural **imperialism**/**hegemony**; second, whether the correlation between the process of globalization and American culture

has decisively **perpetuated** the gap <u>that</u> **distinguishes** winners/dominators from losers/the oppressed <u>or</u> gradually ensured the realization of a global utopia; and third, what lessons are worth learning in a view <u>that</u> American culture has been imagined as culturally **imperialistic** <u>no matter how</u> acceptable <u>or</u> **convincible** it appears. In a world <u>that</u> is getting "smaller", American culture is nothing less than one <u>that</u> has been equally influenced by globalization, whether regarded as a "bandwagon" or "**juggernaut**", as others have. Hence it is not cultural **homogenization**, which proves **unacceptable** <u>because of</u> **undermining** the present **globality** that **exists** and serves as a pillar of globalization, but **competitive** co-**existence** among cultures with an approach to human friendliness <u>that</u> facilitates the process of globalization. In that sense, a positive and constructive attitude towards American culture, which closely refers to American value, language and technology, will help give a profound understanding of the relationships between globalization <u>and</u> the U.S. in terms of cultural factors.

本例中粗體字部份對於初學者可算是生、難字，唸的時候應放慢速度。文中的標點斜線（／，英文稱之為slash），唸法不一，但是依本文文意，建議把斜線當成or這個字，也就是說，一旦看到了斜線，就讀or。

倒數第八行後面的exists既然可能已經放慢了速度，字本身很短，發音也短，所以雖然後面緊接著有連接詞and，就不需要再做停頓了（因此這裡的and並沒有劃底線）。

作業想定之三

　　比照作業想定之二的模式，將練習5的例文讀兩遍（假定您已經明瞭了文意）。第一遍請自行找出發音不易的生、難字，第二遍請在底線詞彙的前面停頓半秒。

　　To describe the problem we face today, I would like to quote what Charles Dickens wrote, "It was the best of times; it was the worst of times." The good news is we've had a lot of colleges and universities, more than expected. If we have enough money, enough time, and strong will, then go ahead. The doors are open. The thing is, when it matters not much to us <u>because</u> there are too many open doors, then why do we have to keep them? For those who work and live on these doors, that could be a bad news. An idea that could be taken into account by the **government** is to **dismantle** some doors of our higher education system. Maybe we can take it more seriously to have more doors closed, not to simply have more doors smashed. So, my points are, first, taking measures to close colleges will **violate** policy consistency, for it is the M.O.E. <u>that</u> welcomed

more schools to appear as <u>or</u> get promoted to colleges or universities; second, the market decides what colleges or universities will survive <u>because</u> it is a matter of supply and demand, so the M.O.E. needs to do nothing but let go; and thirdly, due to the rule of law, no **government** agencies or departments should have any lawfully operated colleges close down.

　　例文中第八行末尾，those和who之間，拼字和發音都很短暫，所以無須停頓。第十行前端，idea和後面緊接的that也有類似情形，不需要停頓。然而倒數第七行中間，appear as視為個別詞組，要放在一起唸，和後面的get promoted to形成對照，因此仍需要在or的前面稍作停頓。

THINK TWICE

It is a myth that being able to speak fast is the hallmark of an orator. Native speakers can always speak extremely fast whenever necessary. That is an advantage they deserve because the mother tongue used and the culture imbedded have long been internalized as a part of their life. But how come not all native speakers turn out to be orators?

A conference presenter does not have to be an orator. He/she is, in an audience's eyes, more like a message conveyor, language performer, fact interpreter, and idea enlightener. No matter what the presenter does, the common ground is how to send signals to the audience effectively and efficiently on the spot. Like the wings that bolster an airplane, fluency and accuracy are usually taken as indispensable to the presentation process, both of which have not much to do with an expression speed-up. Because of the wings well designed and constructed, the plane works well and fly high. In other words, it is fluency and accuracy, not velocity, which facilitate a conference presentation where both the presenter and the audience feel satisfied since the former is clearly understood at a steady pace.

We might wonder why the comma and the period appear most frequently in a text. Where there is a punctuation mark, there is a pause. It serves as a short break during which the readers or listeners will be able to think. On that basis, a friendly presenter tends to take it seriously

to give a timely pause, so the audience will feel easier to think and follow. According to the *Merriam-Webster Dictionary*, fluency means the ability to speak easily and smoothly. Although a fluent speech may sound fast, that is just the effect, not the cause.

英語文小叮嚀

在會議英文的場合進行口頭發表，遇生字或難字時，寧慢勿快，風險較低，切勿逞強。當需要深入分析或評論某些內容時，最好也是放慢速度，不要貪快，快則容易出亂子。身為講者，正確的態度應該是一面思索，一面發言，不是一味靠著死記硬背的功夫才能上場。萬一背了半天的東西忘記了，或者人家問話卻答不出來，那才是糗中之最。

適時放慢速度還有一項優點，那就是可以爭取思考時間。不只是爭取了講者自己的思考時間，也為聽者爭取了思考和吸收的時間。會議英文不只存在著有聲有形的雙向交流，同時存在著這類聽講之間無聲無息的相互默契。然而整體來看，講者也不能總是說得太慢，否則聽者的注意力和好興致將會流失得很快。總之，發言速度永遠保持穩健，該慢則慢，這樣就對了。

前次提及，西方（特別是美國）文化不尚留白。講

者忘詞或長考，可適量摻入一些有助稍微拖延時間的佐料詞，像是nevertheless, so to speak, what I am trying to say is, you know there are several things we need to address here, 等等。至於是否可以趁此自我解嘲一下，甚至講個笑話，筆者的建議是，最好不要，除非您有十足的把握，確信在場觀眾普遍能夠理解您的幽默。

跨文化小叮嚀

關於說話速度，根據多年觀察，有如下發現：使用拼音文字者講話較快，使用表意文字者講話較慢；人微言輕者較快，位高權重者較慢；幼小者快，年長者慢；女性快，男性慢；客服快，客訴慢；面對熟人快，面對生人慢；緊張時快，平靜時慢。但也不能一概而論就是了。

遇到講話比您快的，不需要跟她／他比快，畢竟快有快的原因，不全然表示對方的語文表達能力比您高強。遇到講話稍慢的，也不必勉強拉快對方速度，如果不趕時間，不妨配合跟著一起慢，因為慢有慢的道理，是否對方語文能力較弱，需要花更多時間去思索或咬字？或者是否對方想要強調某些想法，所以不得不慢一些？

萬一講英文實在快不起來（畢竟不是母語），那要怎樣才好？其實不必擔心，只需掌握六字訣：「可以慢，不要停」，保持平常心，從此便能無往不利。當然，為了引起注意，或者為了講求句讀分明，適時停頓（停頓和因為忘詞所造成的留白是兩回事），有時候也是必要的。

練習07（任務目標：帶動聽者亦步亦趨）

　　筆者剛進大學時，同班同學彼此不熟，有人提議到某同學宿舍煮水餃。兩鍋水餃下去後，其中一鍋才煮一下，餃子很快全浮了起來，熟了；另一鍋，煮了好一會兒，火力全開，餃子不但沒浮起來，有幾顆還沾了鍋。原來，前面那鍋顧鍋的同學，只要看到鍋湯將沸，立刻倒進半碗涼水，一沸一倒，來回數次，不但很快弄熟了水餃，大家吃在嘴裡，亦讚不絕口。另一鍋餃子慢熟就罷了，令人喪氣的是，吃起來口感沒那麼好，有幾顆甚至破了，內餡早已流失。日後每當上台講課，或者參加英文會議，筆者總不禁想起這段往事。或許潛意識裡，我把課堂學生和會議觀眾看成了水餃，而自己就是那顧鍋的廚子吧！

作業想定之一

　　面對想像的會議觀眾（由同學、同事或親朋好友擔任；或由空蕩蕩的教室、書房擔任亦可），用英文講述一則童話故事、個人經驗，或者觀賞影視節目或文學作品之後的心得。在此之前，需要草擬一份口語講稿和五張書面投影片（講稿內容須搭配投影片）。實際上場時，在播放第1、3、5張投影片時，試著用稍微重一點的口吻或比較不一樣的表達方式來演講。

Step 1　草擬講稿和投影片

第1張投影片內容

Everyone gets hungry.

講稿

One day, a crow perched on a tree branch. A slice of meat is held in its beak. A fox under the tree looked up, seemed very hungry, and kept watching the crow.

第2張投影片內容

Who cares a Judas kiss?

講稿

The fox said to the crow, "You are the most beautiful crow I've ever seen in the forest." Hearing this, the crow felt flattered. The fox continued, "People say crows are excellent in singing. May I have the honor to invite you to sing?"

第3張投影片內容

Vanity blossoms but bears no fruit.

講稿

The crow became too proud to curb its passion for showing off. No sooner had the bird opened its beak to sing than the meat dropped out of the beak.

第4張投影片內容

Is it never too late to mend?

講稿

The fox grabbed the fallen meat right away, shouting to the crow: "Thanks a lot!" Then it ran away and disappeared.

第5張投影片內容

Stay humble, and never trust strangers.

講稿

The crow remained surprised and kept its beak wide open. It couldn't believe what had just happened.

Step 2 改編講稿

針對投影片1改編後的講稿

Once upon a time, a crow perched on a tree branch. A slice of meat is held in its beak. **The crow thought, "How lucky I am! It is because I've got the meat; how happy I am! It is because I am going to eat."** [講者握拳，收臂，上下擺動手肘，彷彿舞動翅膀] A fox [停頓半秒] under the tree [停頓半秒] looked up, seemed very hungry, and kept watching the crow.

針對投影片3改編後的講稿

The crow became too proud [停頓半秒] to curb its passion for showing off. **It replied, "Sure, why not? You'll regret if you never hear a crow singing like me."** [講者做出清喉嘴的聲音，假裝要開始唱歌似的] No sooner had the bird opened its beak to sing than the

meat dropped out of the beak.

針對投影片5改編後的講稿

The crow remained surprised and kept its beak wide open. **It said, "I cannot believe this. What's the matter? What am I doing? I want my meat back!"** [講者用兩隻手掌摀著頭，假裝痛苦萬分，好像要哭要哭那樣。]

作業想定之二

比照作業想定之一的練習模式，根據練習6的例文，改編成五小段講稿，分別搭配五張書面投影片。改編講稿時，請用稍微重一點的口吻或者比較不一樣的表達方式來宣講第1、3、5張投影片。

第1張投影片內容

Does vocabulary mean proficiency?

講稿

The authorities concerned will adopt a new English

curriculum for senior-high school students. According to the curriculum, the students will have to **keep in mind** at least **7,000 words to build their** vocabulary [講者提到seven thousand的時候，語氣可以加重一些]. They are expected to be equipped with the ability to **listen, speak, read and write** [講者擺出四個肢體語言，分別象徵聽、說、讀、寫] to an acceptable degree before graduation as well. Then what? Can this measure be **taken** as a guarantee of high proficiency in English among these **young students**?

Students on average nowadays are getting **a little bit** better at listening and speaking, while they are obviously **not that good at** reading comprehension. What seems frustrating is that many of them **cannot even** make up a **full sentence** [講者提到「許多學生甚至連個完整句子都造不出來」的時候，語氣可以加重一些]. **What went wrong? Maybe it's about time to think twice and find out a solution.** [原先的Such a phenomenon leaves much room for discussion云云，顯得有點繞口，所以換個更為通俗而完備的說法]. However, it is worth more attention that "the inability to read and write" is the same as "illiteracy", despite the fact that English education for the youth in Taiwan has achieved great success in **helping them learn how to speak and listen** [原稿稍嫌文

縟，所以改用能讓人一聽就懂的說法].

第2張投影片內容

Literacy matters.

講稿（原文為第三和第四段落，均保持不變）

Will memorizing . . . . [略] / "Make your writing . . . . [略]

第3張投影片內容

Vocabulary alone won't work.

講稿

When local **senior students** [原稿逗點多，意義交錯，容易產生不必要的停頓，所以這裡濃縮成通俗易懂的兩個字即可] start to learn English, they must find it **extremely difficult** to think in the language [講者可強調「極端困難」這兩個英文字]. This is a crucial problem that may decide the way one will be dealing with the language, and it is also a difficulty supposed to be

overcome first. **If one never makes any** effort to get used to English syntax and **never knows how to** feel comfortable with the use of it**, it is very likely that** the more words one memorizes [講者刻意停頓一秒], the more **frustrated** one will become.

If one **has limited** vocabulary, definitely one won't be able to express oneself easily. However, even if one's vocabulary is large enough, **what has that got to do with one's English proficiency**? Or even though one has a small vocabulary, does one care for making the best of it? What's more, does one **care** to read often? [講者可用較重語氣讀care這個字]

第4張投影片內容

Reading helps improve vocabulary.

講稿（原文為第七和第八段落，均保持不變）

Experienced English learners . . . . [略] / If one rarely reads . . . . [略]

第5張投影片內容

Encourage students to read!

講稿

It is very much important to motivate one to keep learning English **by laying emphasis on reading comprehension and reading experience. In terms of that,** how much [講者在說完much這個字，立刻停頓半秒] one has read and understood [這裡再停頓半秒，以便讓觀眾有消化理解的時間] serves as an indispensable factor. Therefore, **in regard to** English **proficiency** [因為前面剛剛用過了in terms of這個詞，為了避免重複，所以這裡直接換成了in regard to；講者在提到proficiency時，口吻可以強一些], **reading-oriented** programs will sound more **valid** to help train and evaluate young students. **They will also prove more** effective [effective這個字也可以唸得重一些] **than just having students memorize as much vocabulary as possible**.

　　會議英文簡報好比一場扣人心弦的球賽，必然有高低起伏的過程。球員需要掌握節拍以克敵制勝，自是無可厚非。但是觀眾更需要的是，輕鬆愉快的看球感受。同樣

地，英文會議觀眾也不願長時間被迫（受到來自講者的有形或無形壓力）去附和或記憶講者疲勞轟炸式的如數家珍。

THINK TWICE

It is usually difficult to tell whether conference presenters are involved in a state of single-mindedness or simple-mindedness when their aim is clear – conveying messages to an audience through *live* demonstration primarily based on a verbal display – with abundant information to be shared. However, is the aim always agreeable by both the message conveyors and the message receivers? Maybe we need to find out what our audience really need if we hope to induce the latter to appreciate and better understand our work.

What matters is that the audience cannot remain attentive if they have to observe a talk or presentation lasting more than 10 minutes (some said 5 minutes). Most sessions at an international conference last between 25 and 50 minutes,

so the challenge to presenters or speech makers is not about how much they will say and demonstrate or how well prepared they will appear but *how to elastically proceed in a presentation*. When the session is too long, and when the information to be presented is too much, in addition to selecting and highlighting the key points, one of the smartest ways is to give the audience *a break* from time to time. Such a break is not exactly an interval within the session. It can be put into seamless practice by (1) a causal talk directly or indirectly concerned with the topic, (2) a quick and plain description or demonstration of the unstressed slide intentionally used to strategically illuminate the next emphatic slide, and (3) a stop to solicit a response from the audience.

The aforementioned "stop for a response", "quick and plain description or demonstration", and purposed "casual talk" are the three methods applied not merely to the avoidance of boredom but to the effectiveness of laying empha-

ses. It is unwise to assume that the audience are always ready to receive everything presented in a session at a conference, especially the long one. Such being the case, they deserve an elastic performance that helps them reach better and more comfortable digestion of the presentation contents.

英語文小叮嚀

　　在大庭廣眾下用口頭發表英文，很難不感到緊張。某些跡象，證明緊張程度很高，例如：說話時出現不由自主的顫音、呼吸急促、胃痛等等。某些跡象，證明緊張程度細微，例如：不斷重複下意識動作（輕拉頭髮、裝可愛、抿嘴、抖腿…等等）、不敢掃視觀眾、講話速度太快、濫用口頭禪等等。

　　幾種被濫用了的英文口頭禪或連結語，排名第一的像是 "all right?" 或 "O.K.?" 以及排名第二的 "you know?"，並不適合用來填補口語當中的留白。前者令人感覺地位不對等，好像老師在跟孩童們上課似的；後者令聽者感到氣餒：「不就都講了，都聽的懂了嗎？怎麼還you know, you know個不停？我看是 "We know, but you don't know." 吧！」

　　還有一種算是廣義的副語言（paralanguage），像是語氣上揚的Uh-huh（嗯哼），聊備一格的well（這個嘛／那個嘛），或者為了爭取時間思索而單獨使用，或者因順勢拉長前字尾音而出現的eh或uh（呃／嗯，例如 but → butta 或 I think that → I think tha-ta）。Uh-huh主要用在「一對一」溝通情況下的聽者，不是講者該有的口吻；well和eh, uh適量用可以，但如果過度使用，會逐漸令聽者感到不耐煩，甚至有點好笑。

跨文化小叮嚀

　　英文會議講者苦心孤詣設計簡報PPT，粉墨登台，唱作俱佳，裝瘋賣傻，拼死拼活，最多不過換得與會觀眾難得幾回聞的笑聲和稀稀落落的掌聲。何況大多數情形下，別說是笑聲了，連掌聲都很稀罕。這說明一種現象：在「一對多」的溝通模式下，現場觀眾由於群龍無首，缺乏共識，機動性差，所以較有制式化、機械性反應的傾向，吸收訊息的能力也較弱。

　　因此，講者需要做好心理建設，一次不能給聽者太多訊息。如果發表時間冗長（超過十分鐘以上），簡報內容繁瑣，那麼寧可多花一些時間為聽者說明主要論點，凸顯具有代表性的例證，並且分析意涵，至於其他內容就不能（也不宜）勉強聽者全盤吸收了。俗話說：「貪多嚼不爛。」鉅細靡遺，往往把講者累個半死，聽者也索然無

味，何必如此活受罪呢？

　　現場觀眾如果忽然出現交頭接耳的小騷動，不一定是因為講者犯了錯，有時更可能是因為講者方才提及的內容突然引起聽者的強烈興趣，或是因為講者拋出的想法有某種爭議性，那麼此時不妨暫停片刻，說句Would you tell me what interests (或interested) you? 或者如果為了議程順暢，也可說Would you please leave it to the Q and A session? Probably some of the points will be made clearer if we let the presentation go on.

練習08 (任務目標：利用圖表畫龍點睛)

　　相信大家有過背誦化學元素週期表的經驗：腦袋一片空白，面對洋洋灑灑的名稱和符號，完全不知從何下手。於是聰明的前輩們發明了口訣，代代相傳，版本不一。或許有些人也逛過畫廊，再不然至少看過某些世界名畫（例如「拾穗者」），佇足半晌，即便看不懂，總想試著品頭論足一番吧？其實這就是人類身為萬物之靈的特色：口訣也好，賞析也好，無非為了尋找意義。圖表本身固然井井有條、簡單扼要，使人一目了然。但是負責解說圖表的會議講者，不能只滿足於浮面陳述簡報投影所呈現的一切內容，而應該有所取捨，除了說明原委，凸顯差異，更要講求效率，創造意義。

作業想定之一

　　下列五個簡例，分別代表五種常見圖表。請從每個例子中，各自找出最值得強調的兩個特徵或數據，並約略解釋一下為什麼它們值得特別強調？

Case 1 - 表格（table）

						February
Mon	Tue	Wed	Thu	Fri	Sat	Sun
1	2	3	4	5	6	7
8	9	10	11	12	13	14
15	16	17	18	19	20	21
22	23	24	25	26	27	28
29						

解釋：1. The dates and the days appear identical in the
      first week.
    2. There are only twenty-nine days in February.

Case 2 - 條狀圖（bar chart / column chart）

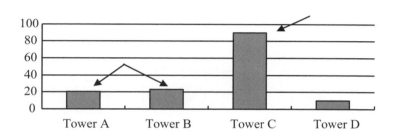

解釋：1. Tower C is the highest building.
    2. Tower A and B appear close in height although
       the latter is higher.

Case 3 - 圓餅圖（pie chart）

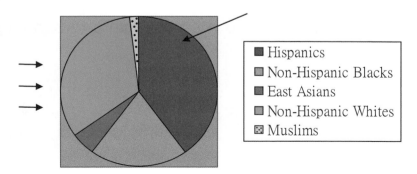

解釋：1. The Hispanics take the largest share in the population.

2. The area to which the chart refers indicates ethnic diversity.

Case 4 - 折線圖（line chart）

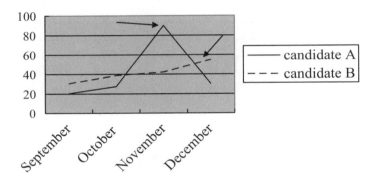

解釋：1. Candidate A reaches the highest approval rating in November.

2. The "golden cross" appears in December between candidate A's nosedive and candidate B's upswing.

Case 5 - 圖解（diagram）

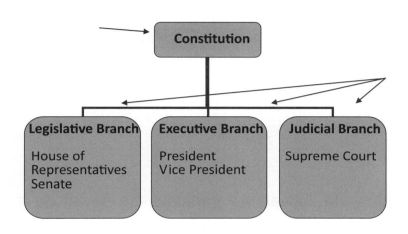

解釋：1. The Constitution guides the government.
　　　2. The government is based on the separation of powers.

作業想定之二

　　根據前次作業想定五大圖例，針對所提到的重點，在口頭方面，各開展出一小段口頭說明；在書面方面，將圖例加入一些必要的佐料（例如：利用不同顏色或字體粗細大小，來凸顯數據或資料上的差異）。

099

Case 1 - 表格（table）

					February	
Mon	**Tue**	**Wed**	**Thu**	**Fri**	**Sat**	**Sun**
1	**2**	**3**	**4**	**5**	**6**	**7**
8	9	10	11	12	13	14
15	16	17	18	19	20	21
22	23	24	25	26	27	28
29						

口頭說明：In Taiwan we translate the seven days of a week like bla bla one, bla bla two, and so on, but Sunday is an exception. So, in the table, the first six dates sound identical and remind me of the days in the week. For example, when it's Thursday, the date is fourth. And Saturday is the same as the sixth. Besides, the table shows twenty-nine days in February; that refers to a leap year, which occurs every four years.

Case 2 - 條狀圖（bar chart / column chart）

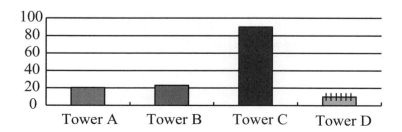

口頭說明：Tower C is located in a city where lands and houses are extremely expensive. Definitely the city is very crowded. On the other hand, the cities where Tower A and Tower B were built are not so crowded as Tower C. Their people's demand for lands and houses is not very strong either. What seems interesting is that the height of Tower A is actually the same as that of Tower B. It is the lightning rod later built that makes Tower B looks a little bit higher.

Case 3 - 圓餅圖（pie chart）

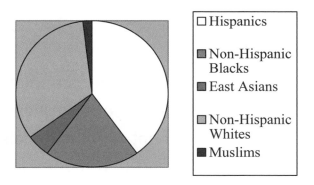

口頭說明：The immigration law has become friendly to illegal immigrants. More and more illegal immigrants, especially those from the nearby Spanish-speaking states, were naturalized as the country's citizens. That's why there is the largest Hispanic population. In

spite of the fact mentioned above, this country is still characterized by its ethnic diversity, where there are whites, the second largest; the blacks, the third largest; and a couple of minorities.

Case 4 - 折線圖（line chart）

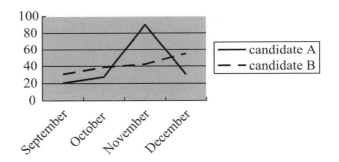

口頭說明：In November, after the campaign debate, candidate A seized an advantageous position he hadn't reached before. However, right after the debate, he was attacked by a series of fraud and money laundering. Next month when he was found guilty, people dumped him. Although candidate B was not a charismatic person, she never made a mistake. She acted like a late bloomer on a slow upswing and was believed to win the election.

Case 5 - 圖解（diagram）

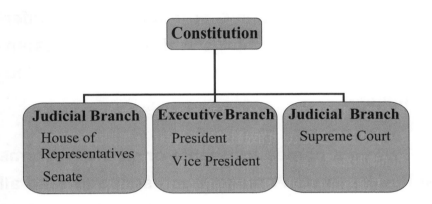

口頭說明：This is a democratic country. The Constitution as the supreme law governs the country substantially. According to the Constitution, the three branches have different functions, and they should work together and supervise each other somehow. Such a game rule in politics is called "checks and balances". Besides, the branches under the rule of law are meant to separate powers, so dictatorship is unlikely to emerge in this country.

THINK TWICE

A pictorial coverage of facts and data is aimed at a clearer and easier display of them. Its oral expression is thus not expected to be per-

formed like a repetition of the coverage as the way it is in a table,chart, or diagram. The conference presenter in charge will have to substantially represent them in a *selective* and *meaningful* manner.

When it comes to a table or whatever forms of figures, it won't make much sense to read all detailed pieces of information from left to right and from top to toe; instead, it will save the energy of all participants to only pinpoint what appears prominent, unusual, remarkable, or/and distinct. The other task a presenter cannot afford to ignore is to interpret what the highlighted parts may mean, such as a further but concise analysis or explanation of similarities and differences, of the highest number/rate and the lowest number/rate, of the largest share and the smallest share, and even of something seemingly shadowed but surprisingly significant.

In short, tables, charts, and diagrams are designed to make the collected facts and data eas-

ily discerned. Their conference presenter should take one more step to get the job done: giving a selective and meaningful interpretation of them.

　　談到圖表，就擺脫不了比較。有時／空的比較，也有人／事的比較。既然如此，有三樣東西用在口頭表達就少不了，筆者以諧音稱之爲「級、時、語」（及時雨）。首先，須能正確運用比較級，例如單音節形容詞比較級用er，最高級用est及是比較級（包括兩音節形容詞以y結尾的分別要用ier及iest），兩音節（含）以上的分別用more及most。

　　其次，須能適切使用時態，尤其容易疏忽的是，同樣發生在過去的兩件事如果彼此出現對照關係，較晚（近）發生的用簡單過去式，較早（遠）發生的用過去完成式。按老美文學界的習慣，引述他人著作時，提到某某人說，某某人主張，某某人指出，某某人斷言等等，可考慮一律以現在式帶過，但如果用法確立下來，就必須保持一致，不可一下現在式，一下過去式。

　　最後，須能正確無誤操作假設語氣。其竅門在於，每當遇到if/provided that/I wish等所建構的子句，先直接看它所用的動詞是簡單過去式還是過去完成式；如果用「簡單過去式」，即可能表達「與現狀不符」，如果用「過去完

成式」，即可能表達「與往事不符」。但仍必須看它所搭配或銜接的另一個子句（除了I wish以外，通常指的是主要子句），其「情狀助動詞」後面所搭配的動詞是以原形的姿態呈現，還是以現在完成式的姿態呈現；如果用「原形動詞」，即表達「與現狀不符」，如果用「現在完成式」，即表達「與往事不符」。

跨文化小叮嚀

　　從事會議英文報告，最忌諱照本宣科；相對地，講者解說圖表，最不該按圖索驥。「驥」既已存在，無需再索；聽者更期待的是，為什麼「驥」在圖裡的長相和姿態會是這樣，而不是那樣。於是乎，有四種頗令觀眾受用的解圖解表技巧，可歸納為四字訣：「尋、人、啟、事」。

　　首先，要給觀眾尋寶的時間，每當投影片一秀圖表，講者先別急著解說，而應該短暫停留數秒，留一點餘地，讓觀眾享受一下找尋意義的樂趣。其次，用擬人化的手法，在詮釋死板冰冷的圖象或表格時，可適量使用令人感覺活潑的動詞，以及具有象徵色彩的名詞。第三，要有啟發性，讓聽者覺得，圖表在經過講者解說以後，有了新的意涵。最後，要有故事性，讓聽者覺得，原來圖表背後也有典故，而且饒富趣味。

　　換言之，圖表只是工具，不是目的。切莫以為花大把時間把圖表弄得漂漂亮亮的，然後站在台上，將圖表裡面

所呈現的數據或事實照著講或照著唸一次，就以為大功告成了。由於一場報告當中可能有許多圖表，個別圖表當中可能也有許多細節，因此會議英文講者在解說的時候，最好還是「擇要」為上，以免效果不彰，對聽者造成某種形式的疲勞轟炸。

　　吟誦專家徐健順指出，今人普遍以為中國以農立國，自古文盲率偏高，然而昔日由於蒙學的普及，老百姓無論識字多寡，仍有一定的文采含量。另有學者指出，古代中國開科取士，既拔擢人才，也普及教育，「寓菁英於平民」，沒當上官的，回頭務農或從商，仍有起碼的讀、算能力。即便如此，過去中國可是千年以上的文明大國。這段史實，讓人聯想起老美薄弱的計算能力，連找個錢都得十元一元的「建構」半天，像這樣的人民，這樣的數學教育，卻造就出一等一的科技強國。走筆至此，意在為（像我這樣）數學不好的人加油打氣，對她／他們來講，能將數據化繁為簡，多麼讓人歡喜。

作業想定之一

　　請運用「取譬法」、「換詞法」和「指義法」，改寫下列案例講稿。「取譬法」是用譬喻的方式來詮釋文中數據，「換詞法」是用不同的講法來解釋原來的數據，而「指義法」則是直接指向數據背後真正的意涵。

　　In 2013, in this city, there were 334 people killed in car accidents. Almost all accidents resulted from drunk driving. Among the victims, 189 people were motorcycle riders, 91 were bicycle riders, 42 were pedestrians, and 12 were car drivers. Although the city mayor and his team

have attempted to stop drunk driving, the accidents it caused still increased twice in the past 3 years. They were just advised to adopt a policy on the alcohol tax. A similar measure that had been taken in the state capital for months proves working to lower the liquor consumption rate.

取譬改寫版：

The year 2013 was a peaceful year to our country. In that year, there was no war; there were no natural disasters either. Only 3 people were killed because of military action overseas against transnational organized criminals. But can you imagine this? Just in the same year, in this city, the people killed by drunk driving were more than one hundred times the number of the overseas casualties. <u>It sounds like having had more than a hundred military operations overseas and 3 soldiers being killed in each</u>. In those accidents caused by drunk driving, most bike riders and pedestrians were killed. In general, people who ride a bicycle or motorcycle and those crossing the road are more vulnerable to traffic accidents, but such vulnerability was found worse in drunk driving. That's why the city leaders have been trying to stop it. However, <u>their attempt is like fighting against the juggernaut, and the juggernaut fought became much stron-</u>

ger in the past 3 years. Will the new idea work? Will potential drunk drivers care if the alcohol tax is levied? Well, the answer may sound hopeful.

第一句的a peaceful year以及第二句的no war和no natural disasters用來鋪陳稍後即將出現的轉折口吻。第三句的military action overseas用來做為取譬的伏筆。第五行的one hundred times as many 是取譬的跳板。

取譬是一種類比手法,旨在提供閱聽想像空間,把抽象的數字概念轉換成具體的事件形象,予人鮮活的感受。一般來說,以數據為基礎,說明事實,則取譬宜採明喻(simile)手法,其特徵在於使用介系詞like,把兩件看似無關,本質上卻有某種相似性的對象,聯結在一起。

按常理,到國外打仗,抓跨國犯罪集團份子,危險性應不亞於交通事故。首譬想像中的數據比對,恰恰顛覆了觀眾的普遍認知。尾譬fighting against the juggernaut明喻螳臂擋車(螳螂所擋之車變強,指酒駕不減反增),一方面彰顯酒駕肇事的嚴重性,另一方面諷喻市政府過去幾年的禁制措施成效不彰。

換詞改寫版:

In 2013, in this city, over three hundred people were killed in car accidents. In other words, they were killed

either in or by drunk driving, if not exaggerated. <u>Over 55 percent of the victims were motorcycle riders; 27 percent were bicycle riders; 12 percent were people walking in the street or those crossing the road.</u> The city mayor and his team have been trying hard to figure out how to curb drunk driving. <u>In the past 3 years</u>, the result was unsatisfactory: <u>the number of traffic accidents caused by drunk driving has doubled!</u> A new policy like having the citizens pay a high price for liquor consumption is being taken into consideration now.

　　換詞就是換個講法，換湯不換藥。為了讓觀眾好記，使聽者易懂，與其講出334這樣太過精細的數字，不如給個大略的數量（over three hundred）。原稿後續一連串數字對講者有意義，對聽者很無趣。如果不想隨便帶過，那麼就換個比較簡略的說法。

　　以上列改寫版為例，當講到over 55 percent，聽者很快會想到「超過半數」；當提及27 percent，聽者很快就能聯想：「喔，這又比剛剛少了一半」；當說出12 percent，聽者馬上會告訴自己：「好像又再少了一半以上」。相較之下，原稿91, 42, 12等三個數字，完全沒有經過適當的說明或轉化，對聽者毫無意義（他／她們當然也沒有義務去記誦那些數字）。

　　原稿文末的increased twice聽來較為文謅謅的，但由

於twice兼有「兩次」和「兩倍」的意思，怕是會引起不必要的困惑，所以改寫版就用了 has doubled，更顯得直接而有力，唯前面記得要配套地補上the number of這幾個字。

指義改寫版：

This city has suffered from a lot more traffic accidents in the past 3 years. All was almost caused by drunk driving. The death toll was surprisingly high. According to the most updated data, motorcycle riders, bicycle riders, and pedestrians are the most vulnerable victims [停頓半秒] who separately take the first, the second, and the third place. Few car drivers were killed. The result shows a relatively lower risk a car driver has to take if he or she chooses to drive despite being drunk. It also explains why it's extremely hard to decrease the number of traffic accidents caused by drunk driving. Therefore the measures that have been adopted and put into practice by the authorities concerned [講者停頓半秒] appear irrelevant [再停頓半秒] and propel the city mayor to take more seriously the alternative measure that has proven effective in curbing drunk driving. The alternative is called [停頓半秒] the liquor consumption tax. Potential drunk drivers would probably never learn, but they do care about the money they've earned.

　　上述講詞幾乎沒有出現任何與酒駕致死相關的數據，而是直接挑明申論其背後意涵。畫底線的部份，都是原稿數字本來沒有的意思，卻是聽者真正想要知道，有助於理解題旨，而且久久不會忘懷的內容。

　　除了先前講次所提過的口語停頓技巧和時機，本例凡是出現較長句型、發音稍嫌繞口，或是有重要名稱的情形，口頭上均應該做出無形的句讀。

　　「取譬」、「換詞」和「指義」等三法，好用，有趣，各有千秋，其中以「指義」為最難，最精粹，也最洗鍊。筆者意在言外的是：會議英文講者上台之前，將所有要講的內容，準備精熟，不過只完成半套流程。至於後半套，講者應該好好思量，細細審度，用最能契合觀眾期待的方式，來呈現已經準備好的講詞。

作業想定之二

　　根據下列簡報投影片的內容，草擬口頭解說，分別運用「取譬法」、「換詞法」和「指義法」，各造兩個英文句子。

投影片內容

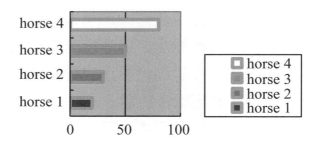

口頭解說版本一（取譬）：

If I were betting on horse racing, I wouldn't place my money on horse 1. If I were crazy, I wouldn't place a bet on horse 4.

此處講者就近取譬，以自己為例，幫助聽者融入情境，彷彿說故事那樣，既烘托了第一匹馬的弱，也婉言了第四匹馬的強。雖然完全沒提到數據，但是已基本上掌握住重點。

口頭解說版本二（換詞）：

The win rate difference between horse 3 and 4 is around 25 percent. A similar situation is found between horse 2 and 3.

　　此處講者從異同之比較入手，雖然並未直接講明諸馬勝算的數字比例，還是能夠令觀眾意識到，第二、第三和第四匹馬之間，以第二匹勝算最低。由於講者意在「擇要」，所以完全不提另一匹勝算更低的馬（house 1）。

　　口頭解說版本三（指義）：

Horse 4 is the one with the best chance to win out. The odds are obviously against the rest of the horses.

　　講者極為乾脆，直接挑明：唯有第四匹馬勝算最高，其餘的馬，沒什麼勝算。此處完全沒有提到任何數據。唯有徹底理解圖表數據的內在意涵，才能做出精簡而犀利的陳述。

　　即便作業想定範例中極少提及數據（都沒直接提），講者仍不應忽略必要的肢體語言。例如：講者可用手勢、指示棒，甚至雷射光筆，往圖表數據相關位置比劃一下，但不必刻意畫圓，更不可劇烈晃動，以免造成視覺混亂，抵銷了肢體語言的效果。

THINK TWICE

Numbers function to count and calculate, while language is a carrier through which the

meanings are coded and decoded. That is to say, language can explain numbers, but numbers do not explain the meanings implied. When presenting statistics at a conference, you'd better figure out how to further explain them.

Besides pinpointing what appears prominent, unusual, distinct,or/and remarkable, the way how you explain the statistics is of equal-importance. First, you should describe the numbers and figures in your own words. Second, you are welcome to interpret them in a creative (not necessarily unfamiliar) manner, including the use of literary techniques of writing, which helps to impress the audience. Thirdly, since numbers are generally seen as boring and not easy to comprehend, you need to, if possible, specify the derived meanings embedded in them.

When it comes to statistics demonstration, the conference presenter should always be thought of as a translator whose job is to transform numbers into language and to introduce

the implications found in such a transformation. A friendly presenter will never ask his/her audience to count or calculate.

　　英字數字不容易唸，比中文囉嗦。一到十還不成問題，只有七（seven）是兩音節；十一到九十九，差不多是兩到三個音節，和中文音節數目相當，也還好。但是成百上千之後，那種發音麻煩的程度，就像滾雪球那樣，愈滾愈大。

　　任舉一例：一年大約365天，中文講三百六十五，音節只有五個；英文three hundred and sixty five卻多達七個音節。那麼試試7,777，中文頂多七個音節，而英文seven thousand seven hundred and seventy seven，音節竟多達十四個，整整多了一倍！所以讀友們如果打開英語新聞聽老外報那斯達克指數蝦咪碗糕的，幾乎聽不懂，跟不上，那是很正常的。

　　或許您會想，以英文為母語的老外也是人，怎麼他／她們就跟連環炮似的說數字，聽數字，算數字，好像沒事一樣？其實英文數字裡面有機關的。有沒有注意到，從後面往前數，每三個數字就會用一個逗點隔開？第一逗，名曰thousand（千）；第二逗，名喚million（百萬）；第三

逗，名叫billion（十億）；第四逗，名為trillion（萬億）。

　　咱們不是做大生意的，手上也不掌握國家預算，那麼最多用到第三個逗點就很夠嗆了。今後請記得，念到英文數字，一旦看見逗點，就直呼其名，只要聽到thousand, million或billion，就想到它們的金額位置（原則上在每個hundred之後都加and）。來，再試試！唸唸看333,333,333，如果念順了，水啦！萬一念的卡卡，建議再接再厲〔正解是three hundred and thirty three million three hundred and thirty three thousand three hundred and thirty three〕。

跨文化小叮嚀

　　從跨文化溝通角度看，西方（尤其有濃厚基督新教色彩的歐美國家）文化有三大特色，一是論理時，追求普遍性（universalism），二是處事時，著重單序性（monochronicity），三是示意時，傾向低境性（low context）。

　　普遍性流露在對於真理（包括宗教、科學和政治等領域）的想望與執著，擅長抽象思考，接受客觀秩序；單序性流露在待人接物的標準方法與一貫流程，按步就班，守時盡份；低境性流露在自我表現的淺層龜毛與深層孤僻，單刀直入，尊重個體。

　　即便如此講求普遍性、單序性和低境性的西方觀眾，初看數字時，一樣感到頭皮發麻。會議英文講者提供數據

資料給現場觀眾，不是只有用手比劃一下圖表，唸唸上面的阿拉伯數字或百分比就算了。聽者需要的是這些數據所代表的意義。講者提供豐富數據，如果缺乏有意義的說明和比較，充其量讓觀眾覺得「他很用功，但又怎樣（so what?）」。

　　因此，假定您身處英文會議場合，面對投影片裡一堆洋洋灑灑的數字，應該努力向觀眾解釋「為何／why」（普遍性）、「如何／how」（單序性）和「幾何／how many or how much」（低境性）。既然應用了人家的語言，理當借用人家的文化思維，把人家語文的優勢和潛在效用發揮到極致，如此，您的會議英文能力才真正「走的出去」。

練習10（任務目標：拿捏影片撥放時機）

　　在YouTube還不是那麼蓬勃發展的年代，校園之間在某個短暫時期，曾經低調流行過一種陋習，那就是在課堂上播放影片。比較有節制的老師，頂多在學期結束前，進度已經結束的前提下，放一整堂課片子；比較誇張一點的，就常常放，美其名曰影視教學，其實難脫殺時間之嫌。直到政府三令五申尊重著作權，加上優酷、土豆等眾多影片流通網站如雨後春筍般興起，「放影片」變的不稀罕，而且有觸法之虞，這股歪風才自行退散。令人敬謝不敏的是，很多學生（包括研究生在內）做英文口頭報告時，常會夾帶幾段影片；這些影視片段雖然跟題旨息息相關，在筆者看來，卻是可有可無。

作業想定之二

　　請用中文寫下，哪五種可能情境會讓您在發表會議英文之時，非放影片不可？其次，請分別至少用一個英文句子，解釋原始動機。第三，請分別至少用一個英文句子，顛覆或否定原始動機。最後，請再分別用至少一個英文句子，簡略說明可能的替代方案。

【參考情境一】遇到不容易用英文解釋的觀念或現象。

原始動機：If I fail to explain the concept or phenomenon which I've found difficult, I am afraid the audience will cast a doubt on my profession and English proficiency. Oftentimes videos

make it much better than I do.

否定理由：It is not the video but the presenter that is expected to give explanations. If I let the video do it, it will be like inviting another person to share the presentation task with me.

替代方案：When I am trying to handle whatever appears incomprehensible, I should spend much more time and make all possible efforts to look it up in useful references.

【參考情境二】需要解釋程序或步驟。

原始動機：I believe that playing videos will help show my audience what the stages really are and how the process exactly goes. "To see is to believe," isn't it?

否定理由：If the steps or procedures I am showing are very complicated and not easy to understand, it would be fine to use a video. If not, why should I leave the job to the video?

替代方案：I will rephrase what the video says, describe the way how it shows the steps or stages that seem complicated, and transform it into something which can be briefly shown and easily understood on certain slides. Of

121

course I will help express all these orally in my own words.

【參考情境三】為了帶動氣氛，誘發觀眾思考。

原始動機：When I talk, my audience can only listen. It doesn't make much sense to have them watch me and the slides all the time. Videos work better sometimes.

否定理由：If videos work better, why am I here as a presenter? If most members of the audience do not get inspired by or pay attention to me or my slides, why are they here?

替代方案：If I have to apply some videos to my presentation for guiding my audience, I will limit the use of them. If I don't have to use any, I will request my audience to do something, such as thinking twice on a debate or answering questions.

【參考情境四】自覺口頭報告內容太短或準備不周。

原始動機：No matter how short my oral presentation appears, or no matter how unprepared I am for it, videos are believed to kill time and leave no blanks.

否定理由：I am wasting my audience's time if I choose not to present myself but to play videos too often or too much without giving any acceptable excuses.

替代方案：I should enrich my presentation with further analysis and more evidence. If possible, I can have a dialog with my audience when presenting my stuff. I can also choose to extend the Q&A session if my presentation is finished earlier than expected.

【參考情境五】覺得影片內容比我的口條更清楚、更有趣。

原始動機：The video clip I quote overwhelm me. I guess my audience will feel the same. They probably will thank me for showing something interesting or creative of that sort.

否定理由：If the video quotes are found more interesting or creative, that seems not bad. However, it could be like inviting some eloquent speakers to compete with me. I can't win. There is no need to compete. As a presenter, I should be in charge.

替代方案：If the videos are believed to be very helpful and inspirational, I won't play them in my

presentation but tell my audience, through a slide show, how and where to access those videos.

相對而言，由於主要從觀眾立場著眼，前列參考情境以一、二和三較屬情有可原。參考情境四最為常見，卻最不可取。參考情境五看似為觀眾著想，其實等於把講者口語表達的責任推給影片，行為仍不可取。

作業想定之一

根據下列個案，各草擬一段英文說詞，旨在說明影片播放緣由（假定尚未放片）；另再各草擬一段英文說詞，旨在補充說明或議論影片內容，但不能偏離講者報告本身的題旨（假定剛播放完影片）。

Case 1 - 我想跟觀眾介紹美國總統選舉的機制，剛好網路上有一段動畫短片，線條簡單，色彩分明，可以讓我的解說得到充分支援。

播片前：One of the things Taiwan and the U.S. have in common is that they both are characterized by the Presidential system. In Taiwan, the system is based on "one man, one vote" in a general election. In America, the general election goes first, but the second stage is much more decisive. The ballots given by the Electoral College will decide who wins the Presidential election right after the general election. That is, the popular votes collected in the general election are to be converted into the electoral votes. Actually *the whole process is very complicated*. For example, the congressional seats, including those from the Senate and from the House of Representatives, will be taken into account. There also exist exceptions like the state of Nebraska and the state of Maine, where the electoral votes calculation do not follow the rule of "The winner takes it all". I am sure you won't get confused if we choose to understand, step by step, how the system goes. Now let me show you a video clip which lasts only 30 seconds. *I searched and found it at YouTube. The filmmaker is an American young scholar who has been devoted to the studies of U.S politics for years at Stanford University.*

播片後：The short video focuses on the difference between the popular votes and the electoral votes. Then it highlights the conversion formula that helps viewers understand how the popular votes are translated into the electoral votes. Because the winner takes it all, during the campaign, most candidates tend to stay longer in the states where there is a much larger population. What's more, the system can also be seen as a metaphor that explains American fed-

eralism. The seats each state is allowed to have in the Senate are always two. The number means a lot to the states where there is a smaller population in terms of the electoral votes.

Case 2 - 我想跟觀眾解釋何謂onomatopoeia（擬聲詞），剛好網路上有段動畫PPT，條理清晰，例證精彩，可以讓觀眾更加理解我的說明。

播片前：Onomatopoeia means the imitation of sounds. It also means whatever word made to imitate a sound. To imitate a sound, you need to spell a word that helps to deliver it. For example, buzzing is the word created to represent noises made by bees. Now it also has been used to identify with machine noises or the like. "Wow" is more direct. It is an exclamation that expresses surprise or wonder. Once again, please listen up: ono—mato—poe—ia. Not easy to read, right? But it's quite interesting to know more about how it has been applied to our everyday practice. *The video I am going to show you was uploaded and shared by a group of language experts living and working in the U.S. When you watch it, it'll be fun if you take some notes. That will prove helpful when we reach the Q&A session.*

播片後：So, how does it feel? What have you found? I didn't mean the background music, which is not what I really expected. [若干觀眾可能有笑聲] Have you found any common grounds that make an onomatopoeia meaning-ful? [講者停頓五秒，但不是真的要聽取觀眾回答，而是要誘使觀眾去思維] You can explore every onomatopoeia closely through its word origin. My point, like what some of the examples given by the videos suggest, is that onomatopoe-ias are not simply a by-product in a language. They imply different stages of civilization. They also reflect humans' worldview. There are two among the most prominent ex-amples. You wouldn't have said "beep" before the 20th century. And the word "click" was not used and understood in the same manner as it is now.

Case 3 - 我想讓觀眾體會1960年代民權運動的氛圍，但我主要還是為了說明當時美國年輕一代，不分族群，希望國家更多元、更美好。

播片前：Living in a society that has been culturally diverse in many aspects, you just cannot imagine how des-perately American young people longed for true freedom five decades ago, the freedom best described by mutual tol-erance and cultural reconciliation. These young guys now

become very old, but the dream they've been pursuing is still new and will never fade away. *The video* that I am going to quote here will not take too much time. It *is a part of the speech made by Martin Luther King, Jr.* [Jr.唸Junior], *which* I believe *will help you witness their passion for a much better democracy, although you were not there. What is more worth your attention in the video is the crowd in the assembly.*

播片後：Did you see that? *Young people who had come from different places got together at that moment for the same goal. They were blacks, Asians, whites, Latinos, and so on. They were smiling to their hero* onstage. I would say Martin Luther King was not just that man speaking for himself. He was the man *who spoke for the world.* If you had been among the crowd then, Dr. King's words of wisdom would have felt like sparks of hope, shedding on you and on the generations to come.

THINK TWICE

A video is an animated display of information supported by audio and pictorial arts. It is supposed to play a minor or subordinate role

at a conference where presenters express their ideas *live*. As for the presenters, such impromptu-like performance makes self-evident that they are prepared to talk and ready to take action in accordance with how their audience respond.

Videos won't talk. They cannot judge the hour and size up the situation either. That is why when a conference presentation is found full of videos or occupied by a lengthy video, it could feel like a fraud. Before having to play any videos, a shrewd presenter will sufficiently explain their contextual relevance, such as how important they are to the presentation topic, why they are worth watching in such a presentation, and what is expected to be featured.

Therefore, at a conference, videos should only be taken as a visual aid. If a presenter insists on playing videos too often or playing them more than enough, he/she could become an aide to them. The average audience would rather see one strive and struggle onstage than observe a tail wag its dog.

　　假使這是一場為特定專業領域人士所舉辦的英文會議，通常不太可能另闢時間為現場觀眾解說專有名詞。同一場會議，假如所邀請的觀眾來自四面八方，並不侷限於特定專業，那麼講者就算沒有時間解釋專有名詞，至少應盡可能以較為生活化的方式，來表述本來想要用在口頭報告裡的生澀字眼。

　　承接前述情境。如果所用詞彙相當專業或偏門，數量又不少，那麼講者可慮列出一張解釋名詞清單，在資源允許的前提下，複印幾份給現場觀眾參考。或者講者可自行判斷，挑選一至三個最具代表性的專有名詞，稍微多作解釋，其餘偏冷詞彙則略去不用，僅列在投影片中聊備一格，口頭上則改以平易方式詮釋相關概念。

　　當專業講者遇上通俗聽者，應秉持從易到難，由淺入深，自簡至繁的發言原則。當專業講者面對專業聽者，後者會更關注前者發言內容的原創風格與特殊賣點。總的來說，除非為佐證所必須，身為英文會議講者，影視片段還是少放為妙；放多了，只會減損講者的原創性，令觀眾麻痺而抓不著重點。

　　「放影片」這種事情沒有好壞對錯，主要是看時機、作用、對象和場合是否恰當。影視片段（包括自己拍攝的在內）的在各類英文會議所扮演的角色，充其量就像是書

籍裡面的「引文（quotes）」和「註解（notes）」。徵引過當，則主客易位；註解浮濫，則輕重不分。動輒撥放影片，一不小心，常能破壞會議報告的完整性，甚至打亂講者自己的節拍與步調。如果情非得已，需要利用影視片段，爲口頭發表增色，那麼請留心以下三件事情。

首先，影片本身的音效和文字要符合會議語文的基調。除非講者要發表的內容涉及文化或文學比較，否則在一場英文會議裡，突然跑出幾段中文影片（或英片中字，或中片英字），會給人格格不入的感覺，觀眾可能因此連帶懷疑講者的專業和英文能力。質言之，所播放的影片內容當中的語言和文字，務必保持一致。

其次，就像在書籍或論文裡面徵引他人著作片段那樣，講者播放影片前／後，必須給現場觀眾提供若干說明、分析或批評，最好能約略解釋一下爲什麼必須播放這段影片、影片攝製的背景、出處和主題關聯性，以及觀眾需要留意的部份等等。換言之，講者務必有目的，有準備，有選擇的播放影片，不能無的放矢，更不可藉此消磨時間。

最後，影視片段的內容應淺顯易懂，不宜嘈雜喧鬧，更不宜過度吸睛或引發爭議，以免蓋過會議報告本身的風頭（或講者的風采）。換言之，引用影片時，務必有所取捨。講者再怎麼準備不周，再怎麼緊張萬分，就算與現場觀眾東扯西聊，甚至進行即時討論，其效果都要好過播放一顆「可能會弄壞整鍋粥」的「老鼠屎」。

練習11（任務目標：使令觀眾回心轉意）

昔日在某高商兼課，學生程度頗差，學習動機低落。隔壁班老師特兇，有時遠遠就能聽到他／她們大喊「不要講話」。這四個字，筆者發現效果有限，最多就是從「我講我的，他講他的」變成「我講我的，他不講了」。筆者有位三十多年交情的老友，著作等身，以前也教過程度不好的學生。差別在於，他特會耍幽默，並且懂得恩威並施。在他「治下」的班級，就算沒有脫胎換骨，總還可以服服貼貼的看著他上課。多年以後，自己有了小孩，偶然聽見擁有多年幼教經驗的老師提醒：「跟孩子講話，請他／她一定要看著你！」這才警覺到，「凝視」在口語交流過程中，不可或缺。

作業想定

請準備好一份英文簡報（主題不拘），重在口語發表，PPT可做可不做。然後依循下列題旨，採取行動，並填寫答案。

* Invite a partner to work with you in the imagined situations below, where you are requested to solve a problem. On one hand, as the presenter, you will evaluate your own performance after the presentation. On the other hand, the partner will observe your performance and give a short comment. If possible, please take turns playing each other's roles. You and your partner are also encouraged to compare each other's comments or/and evaluations.

Situation 1: At an international conference, you are going to make a presentation that lasts at least 10 minutes. Most of your audience is very good at English. Many are native speakers from English-speaking countries.

〈背景〉台下觀眾以講英文的老外居多。

〈提示〉兩不：講者勿過度自謙，勿隨意道歉，以免令自己表錯情，讓聽者會錯意。講者應該禁用如下句型：

My English is very poor. / I know not much about this topic. / I feel sorry to waste your time. / You know more about this than I do.

〈提示〉兩要：講者若口說能力弱，速度慢，思考久，不如「逼」自己說快一些，容許文法錯誤，但是邏輯要正確。講者若口說能力強，速度夠快，思考敏捷，更應該要時時保持與觀眾之間的目光交流。

Situation 2: This situation is a little different from situation 1. Here most of your audience is not very good at English. Many are non-native English speakers from Asia, Africa, or Latin America.

〈背景〉觀眾多來自「非英語國家」或「非核心英語國家」。

〈提示〉兩不：講者眼神和口吻都不應太強勢。

〈提示〉兩要：同situation 1。

Situation 3: This situation is a little different from situation 2. During your presentation, for unknown reasons, most of your audience is very noisy. Suppose you are in a 100-seat conference hall, and there are only 20 to 30 people sitting scatteredly. Now you are trying to draw your audience's attention back.

〈背景〉觀眾背景多元，但缺乏遵守紀律或尊重講者的意識。

〈提示〉兩不：講者勿視若無睹，勿動氣罵人。

〈提示〉兩要：講者要離開講台，主動出擊。剛開始時，要花少許時間暖身，跟觀眾話話家常，簡單聊聊各自家鄉文化。

Situation 4: This situation is a little different from situation 3. Suppose most of your audience remains silent, but actually they are focusing on their iPads or iPhones while sitting far away from you, how are you going to draw their attention back?

〈背景〉同situation 3。

〈提示〉同situation 3。

Situation 5: This situation is a little different from situation 4. Although most of your audience remains silent, some of them keep yawning; the others continually watch the time. Now you are trying to draw their attention back.

〈背景〉同situation 3。

〈提示〉兩不：講者勿視若無睹，勿亂講笑話（以免引起不必要的文化誤解和衝突）。

〈提示〉兩要：講者既要提高音量，簡單總結重點，也要適時離開講台，走近觀眾。

Situation 6: Your presentation takes place in a medium-sized room, where there is a large number of audience. Although your profession seems unfamiliar to most of the audience, you will have to finish the presentation within 10 minutes. In general, there is no problem with the use of English between you and your audience.

〈背景〉講者只能利用短暫時間，向觀眾介紹他／她們所不熟悉的專業知識。

〈提示〉兩不：講者態度不要太嚴肅，說話步調不要太急切。

〈提示〉兩要：講者要說重點，且要儘量使人感到通俗易懂。

    * Invite a partner to work with you in the imagined situations below, where you are requested to talk in a prescribed way. On one hand, as the presenter, you will evaluate your own performance after the presentation. On the other hand, the partner will observe your performance and give a short comment. If possible, please take turns playing each other's roles. You and your partner are also encouraged to compare each other's comments or/and evaluations.

Situation 1: At an international conference, you are going to make a presentation that lasts at least 10 minutes. Now you are in a very large hall, and it is crowded with the audience. Actually there is not much space for you to move close to any member of the audience, and the stage where you stand is a little higher than where your audience sits.

〈背景〉會場雖大,但觀眾也多。講者只能待在講台,位置稍高於台下觀眾。

〈提示〉兩不:講者聲音不要太小,音調則不必太高亢。

〈提示〉兩要:講者說話速度要穩,但肢體動作幅度要大。

Situation 2: In situation 1, if your partner feels the oral pitch you used in the presentation is too high to sound like talking to an individual member of the audience, please do the presentation one more time, trying to use a lower pitch. However, if your partner feels your pitch is low enough in situation 1 to sound like talking to an individual, then you don't have to do it again but directly go on to situation 3.

〈背景〉同situation 1。

〈提示〉同situation 1。

Situation 3: This situation differs from situation 1 in its few members of the audience. What's worse, they choose to sit far away from the stage where you stand. Now you are trying to use the lowest pitch to draw their attention to your 10-minute presentation.

〈背景〉會場很大，觀眾卻很少。講者位置稍高於台下觀眾。

〈提示〉兩不：講者不能只待在台上，不要假裝有眾多觀眾。

〈提示〉兩要：講者要輪流走近散坐在台下的觀眾，此時肢體動作幅度要小一些。

Situation 4: If situation 3, if your partner feels your pitch is too low to sound normal, please do the presentation one more time to improve yourself. If there seems to be

nothing wrong, please go on to situation 5.

〈背景〉同situation 3。

〈提示〉同situation 3。

Situation 5: This is an experimental situation. Now you are ready to make a 10-minute presentation in a very small room, where there are only 12 seats. What surprises you is that 13 people are showing up to join you. One of them is willing to stand during your presentation. When doing the presentation, you try to use the highest pitch and see how your audience will react to it. After completion of task, if you and your partner feel stupid or weird, please figure out why you feel that way and add the answer to your comment or evaluation.

〈背景〉會場很小，觀眾人數卻略多於座位容納量。

〈提示〉講者刻意用最高的音調說法，同時觀察自己的感受和觀眾的反應。〔本情境屬實驗性質，僅供小組互動參考。〕

Situation 6: Your 10-minute presentation will take place in a very big room, where most of the seats are empty. There are only about 8 to 12 people staying to watch the presentation. What surprises you is that they all choose to sit in the first row, obviously close to you.

The stage where you stand is a little higher than the audience seats.

〈背景〉會場很大,講台位置稍高於觀眾席。觀眾雖少,卻坐在離講者最近的一排座位。

〈提示〉兩不:講者不要停留在一個定點過久,更不要一下子走上台,一下又走下台(留台上或待在台下,應早做決斷)。

〈提示〉兩要:如果有放PPT,講者就要留在台上(如果沒做PPT,便無此必要,留在台上或待在台下皆無不可)。若待在台上,肢體動作幅度可大些;若待在台下,肢體動作幅度要小些。

THINK TWICE

We as presenters have always emphasized how important it is to key regular eye contact with people to whom we are conveying messages. Even so, we probably haven't paid substantial attention to our audience. When we talk in public, especially in a way oriented by one to many, are we sure most members of the audience keep their eye contact with us too? If they don't bother to, it is not our fault. But if we simply ignore it, the situation may get out of our

control.

At one extreme, our audience may remain indifferent. Many of them could be indulged as phubbers. At the other extreme, they may become very noisy. For us, it is of no use to hurry; it doesn't work to pretend to be passionate either. Just a small step taken will prove effective to kindle the audience's interest: moving toward them. When we approach our audience, the latter will feel unconsciously defensive while behaving on the alert. So the next step to take is to show our friendliness by reiterating the key or selling points of the presentation while looking at them mildly.

By and large, when we stand far away from the audience, we take a general look at them. When we get close to them, we take a selective look at them one by one. However, it could be unwise to focus on whoever sits closest to us because it is likely to offset our friendliness and cause unnecessary tension.

　　希望讓觀眾「聽你的」，是會議英文講者最值得追求的夢想：積極而言，能有效傳遞訊息；消極而言，能有效掌控局面。「老師在說，你有沒有在聽？」一個最容易判別的跡象，是觀眾在「聽你的」之前，有沒有先「看著你」？以下謹拋磚引玉，分享五種簡易手法，用來幫助聽者重新將注意力放回講者身上。

　　一是聚焦法：適用於較大會場，尤其觀眾坐很稀落，或是坐的離講台很遠。此時講者需要保持機動，發言時，不以講台爲唯一歸宿，而是儘可能輪流接近坐在不同區塊的觀眾。

　　二是活絡法：適用於觀眾反應消極，會場氣氛沉悶時。在不偏離主題的前提下，講者或拋出話題，令台下觀眾彼此分享看法；或設計任務，令觀眾現場親自操作。

　　三是暫停法：適用於會場嘈雜失序，或者觀眾反應過於熱烈時。講者或中斷發言數秒，直到觀眾恢復平靜；或直接關閉投影器材，改用板書。

　　四是發問法：做法上，與活絡法有相通之處，在不偏離主題的前提下，講者或提出問題，令觀眾回答；或令觀眾彼此發問，相互答覆，然後講者再加入討論，分享看法。

　　五是閒聊法：適用於較小會場，尤其議程冗長，話題嚴肅，致使觀眾心不在焉時。講者或者話鋒一轉，用閒話

家常的口吻，講講歷史典故或個人經驗；或者短暫偏離主題，談談現場瑣事。

　　強迫灌輸，抑或放牛吃草，皆非究竟良策。若能略施小計，借力使力，講者不必總開口閉的May I have your attention please? Would you please keep quiet? 至於像Would you keep your mouth shut?或Shut up! 這樣的句子，太過強勢，不說爲妙。畢竟，站在「台上」，等同被賦與了POWER，再去跟坐在「台下」的人一般見識，豈不白白便宜了後者？

跨文化小叮嚀

　　自有人類社會以來，就有情境的問題。情境涉及角色扮演、社交投入與物理配置等三大要素。以會議英文情境爲例，聽者和講者，包括串場的引言人，扮演著不同角色，但是出了會場，或許講者私下和某些聽者熟識，而引言人可能是某位聽者的親友，這是不同的角色扮演。會議的宗旨是爲了分享和討論想法，在此社交場合，大家有共同的目標和期待；可能在會後，其中兩位聽眾相約喝咖啡，到了店裡，則是另一種社交局面。會議場所的位置、大小、格局、亮度、溫度、座位安排、布置方式等等，自然指的是物理配置了。

　　已知個案當中，談到物理配置因素的似乎相對較少。君不見，談情說愛，往往選在花前月下？可見物理配置重要之一斑。有一種會議講者，把自己「釘」死在講台或電

腦桌後面；另一種講者，不是橫著走來豎著去，像「小蜜蜂」那樣，搖頭晃腦地左右移動，就像「找不東西又三心二意」那樣。這兩種講者，都很令人著急，不知他／她們自己是否曉得，這麼懼怕觀眾，或者這麼頻繁地挪動身軀，爲的是什麼。

假如會場較大，觀眾偏少，且坐得較開，只要他們願意看著講者，還留在場中，基本上問題不大。假使雖然會場很大，觀眾坐的滿坑滿谷兼水泄不通（無論是否出於自願或被「動員」而來），只要麥克風等器材功能正常，而場子竟然熱不起來，想必是講者或講題太無趣。

早期講者面對大型會議，只要看見現場人多，往往不分青紅皂白，不論手上有沒有擴音器或麥克風，一律用高八度的音調在說話，聽來相當做作；這在今天，恐怕並不合大多數聽者的脾胃。畢竟不是所有的群眾聚會場合都在拼場造勢，也並非所有的大型會議場合都在發表振奮人心的演說。時代已經不同。講者上台展現親和力的不二法門，是把「許多人」當作「一個人」看待，把天邊之遙當成咫尺之近，自自然然就會用比較「正常」的聲音來說話。

練習12（任務目標：處理危機由剝而復）

初任教時，學業未竟，工作未穩，幸虧有機會在北部多所院校兼課。長達六年「周遊列國」的日子，最感謝的是那些被我「教」過的學生。他／她們來自不同年齡層，有著不同的學習背景，提問光怪陸離，令人頗難招架。這些經驗，和許多教師經歷雷同，最尷尬的就是當被學生「問倒了」的時候：我說不會，怎配當人師？我隨便回答，又怎面對良心？筆者死豬不怕開水燙，碰到一時答不上來的，一律回曰：「你的問題很棒。容我想想，過兩天給你滿意的答覆。」曾有人做過民調，教師「有學問」或「會教書」，在您心目中哪個更重要？歐美學生多半選後者，亞洲學生多半選前者；答案頗耐人尋味。

作業想定

請依照下列會議場合可能出現的突發狀況，研擬英文草稿（使用完整句型），提出相應對策或解決方案，並（以中文）評估可行性。

器材故障之一：麥克風沒聲音

【對策／解決方案】If the microphone doesn't work, I will ask the moderator or any other staff members concerned for help. If there is no one who can help, then during my presentation I will have to walk toward the audience to make myself heard more clearly.

【可行性】引言人雖然職責並不在此，但可幫忙尋求外援。現場工作人員通常不一定有能力排除機械障礙（有經驗的，或者機伶一些的行政人員或義工，可能會攜帶備用麥克風）。講者最好自己攜帶備用隨身麥克風，若實在沒辦法，只能走近觀眾，扯開嗓門作報告了。

器材故障之二：電腦當機

【對策／解決方案】If the computer had a bad connection, or if it just crashed, I would ask the staff members for help. If the problem couldn't be solved in a short time, I would have no choice but make my presentation without using any electronic devices. If so, my performance would appear more like an impromptu speech.

【可行性】如果現場人員或義工無法排除問題，臨時又找不到維修技師，除了因此被迫做「即席」發表之外，其實還是有別的解決方法。電腦雖然壞了，投影設備可能是好的！講者如果隨身攜帶筆電，看看能不能把它連接到會場的投影器材；這樣一來，還是可以用到PPT（就怕接線插孔規格不相容）。

器材故障之三：投影機不能使用

【對策／解決方案】This problem is even worse than a crashed computer. First I will try to reset or restart the projector. If it doesn't work, then I will have to present

my stuff without using a PPT file.

【可行性】現代會議演講廳大多已配備能夠連線到（有網路支援的）電腦的新式投影機（overhead projector），那種笨重的古董級投影機（且需要用到真正的投影膠片），現在幾乎看不到了。如果投影機壞了，真的等於提前宣告PPT白做了嗎？不見得。傳統講者會準備多張小卡片，裡面寫滿了洋洋灑灑的筆記重點，用以備忘。現在則不必那麼麻煩。為求保險起見，講者可將PPT內容（或自己平常準備的重點）縮小列印出來（fine print），帶到會場，以備不時之需。

器材故障之四：PPT 檔案不相容或不能用

【對策／解決方案】I will consult the staff members first. But I know usually they won't be able to deal with the problem. The possible causes of my PPT file failure could include virus or Trojan attack, software or USB incompatibility, and whatever else unknown. So, I had better prepare some memo cards or just print out the PPT slides in a smaller size. They may come in handy at the conference

【可行性】對於極度依賴PPT備忘的講者來說，這個問題如果沒有事前「預先」以準備「備忘卡片」的方式來解決，幾乎無解，否則只有把自己的筆電接到會場的投影器材了（萬一規格不相容，依然沒輒）。

空間障礙之一：場外噪音惱人

【對策／解決方案】In that case, I won't stop my presentation but give a meaningful look or gesture to the staff member nearby. If there is no one who can help, then I will have to interrupt my presentation, say to my audience, "Excuse me for a few seconds", walk to the door, open it, step out a little bit, and remind whoever makes noises that a meeting is being held inside.

【可行性】如果現場工作人員訓練有素，這類狀況應可立刻獲得排除。原則上從事會議英文發表，以順暢為先；講者貿然中斷發言，原有的步調與節奏可能會被打亂，聽者的注意力也容易散失。

空間障礙之二：場內悶熱或空氣不流通

【對策／解決方案】In case of the air conditioning problem and the room that feels stifling, I would suggest that my audience open the windows and leave the doors open. If the solution doesn't work, I will keep the minimum lights on only required to satisfy the presentation; hopefully the temperature would get lowered.

【可行性】現代人無法想像，會議廳裡怎麼可以沒有空調。話雖如此，再好的空調，也有故障或冷媒不足的時候。既然無法更換場所，講者和聽眾唯有共同努力降低室溫。現場如果不錄影，沒有採光的需要，那麼除了投影機

147

之外，就算把所有的燈光都關掉也無所謂。但如此一來，觀眾只聽到講者的聲音，看不到講者的肢體動作，而且不方便做筆記。

空間障礙之三：觀眾人數爆滿

【對策／解決方案】An ambitious presenter could be very excited to see a large audience. However, a large audience could cause chaos. If chaos occurs, I will ask the audience to "do something", such as answering my questions, responding to a debatable issue just raised, inviting some of the audience to get onstage working with me, etc. If there is no chaos, one of the most challenging things for me could be how to keep regular eye contact with a large audience like that.

【可行性】在這種情形下，講者要勉強與觀眾時時保持目光接觸，可能並不切實際。除非與觀眾之間個別相互問答，講者大可只是保持目光大略投向觀眾席，以（半）環狀「掃視」的方式，取代真實的目光接觸，肢體動作也可以豐富些。

時間障礙之一：引言人遲到

【對策／解決方案】If the moderator's late arrival is likely to cause a heavier time pressure, I will choose to begin with the presentation without delay. Once I get started, I won't let anyone, including the late moderator, to interrupt me.

【可行性】由於引言人要負責介紹講者背景與略述緣起，如果遲到的話，是很失禮的，所以講者無須為直接進入發表主題而感到內疚。唯講者需要部份吸收引言人的任務，在觀眾面前略作自我介紹，交代主題緣起，可能因此會稍稍耽誤一些正式口頭發表的時間，但總比等在那裡跟觀眾大眼瞪小眼來的好。

時間障礙之二：觀眾遲到

【對策／解決方案】If there is no time pressure, I will wait until more people coming in while having some small talks with the moderator and the staff members. If I am running out of time, I won't wait too long. In that sense, I will also have to make a presentation briefer than planned.

【可行性】觀眾遲到所引發的問題，並非如想像中單純。觀眾如果不是遲到太久，那倒無所謂。如果為數眾多，由於方才錯過了講者說過的東西，可能因此會顯得困惑，甚至不安於位，造成現場秩序紛亂。因為不容易（或尚未）進入狀況，他／她們到了發表結束前的問答階段，甚至可能搖身一變，成為亂問問題的奧客。為避免大家繼續在那裡不必要的「勾勾纏」，講者在做結論的時候，最好能簡要複述重點，為自己打「預防針」，幫觀眾「醒醒腦」。

時間障礙之三：議程拖延致使所剩發言時間不足

【對策／解決方案】If that is the case, I will ask myself , "Which could be the most important part of my presentation? What am I trying to "sell"? If I know what it is, I will explain it to the audience and make it short enough.

【可行性】最佳策略是用一句話闡明主旨或中心思想，然後跳過中間所有流程，直接報告結論。如果可能的話，儘量保留少許時間讓觀眾提問：講者一面回答，一面收尾，也算是留下了一幅賓主盡歡的畫面。

人員障礙之一：腦筋打結忘詞

【對策／解決方案】If I forgot what to say, I would take a quick look at the PPT slide. If there were no PPT, I would skip the part I just forgot and continue with another part which I think is relevant to my discussion.

【可行性】無庸置疑，PPT不只用來引導觀眾，更是拿來備忘的。萬一沒有PPT，那麼趕緊先講還記得的部份。只要講者準備充分，道理清楚，往往時候到了，忘記的部份會再浮現回腦海。

人員障礙之二：講評者出言不遜

【對策／解決方案】If I have to reply at that moment, I'll start with the questions which I can deal with much better. If not much time remains, I'll say "thank you" to my discussant and promise to give an answer later after the meeting.

【可行性】講評人（discussant）通常來自主題相關領域，層級比講者還高。會令講評人說出難聽的話，不外乎：一、在行家眼光下，講者所論，水準不高，問題很多；二、講評人沒有獲得實質應有的回報，或者沒有得到主辦單位應有的尊重，於是直接間接把「氣」出在講者（發表人）身上；三、以上皆是。然而，講者身處知識（權力）和人脈相對弱勢，若遭逢講評人明顯不合理批判（甚至人身攻擊），為了長遠利害，為了就事論事，最好別跟對方一般見識。

THINK TWICE

It is not easy to prepare and hold a conference. Its budget has equal priority in physical contexts such as facilities and equipment maintenance and in social and interpersonal contexts like invitations, receptions, and transportation.

You will find it worthwhile to keep your shirt on when annoyed by any unexpected, usually unpredictable, problems imposed on you during the presentation sessions. To release the

hidden fury, you'd better find someone to talk with, showing your empathy for this undesirable situation. Neither complaints nor quarrels would work but prove you impatient and troublesome. Sometimes the discussant or moderator working with you could be rude and unfriendly. He/she could criticize your presentation in an extremely embarrassing way. If such an attack makes no sense, definitely you are welcome to (and you should) argue. The bottom line is that what you are trying to do is to make things clearer based on facts and reasons in a neutral or euphemistic tone.

When joining a conference and acting as a presenter, you really cannot expect too much of the conference hosts. Nevertheless, there is no reason to feel depressed. It is because your aim is clear: to expose yourself to the public, say something in your own words, and make it as understandable as you can. Sink or swim, it is at your discretion to clear whatever blockades.

　　祈請他人為自己排除障礙或解決問題，第一優先是使用疑問句型，第二優先是使用（簡易的）假設句型，第三優先是使用加了「請」字的使役句型，最等而下之的是使用完全不加請求字眼的使役句型。

　　疑問祈請用法最常見的就是以Would you（please）開頭的句子，像是Would you please do me a favor? 或Would you close the door behind you? Would you show me the way? 簡易假設句型像是We will be very grateful if you can help deal with it. 或是像 I'll be very appreciative of your help if you can do this. 甚至可以將疑問句型與假設句型合併使用，像Would you mind making two cups of coffee for us? Would you mind if I used your computer? 不過，有種聽來取巧，卻也滿令人受用的說法：I am wondering if you will.... 當中的if只能當作whether解釋（意即「是否」，不是「如果」），不能算是假設句型。

　　至於Would you mind if I後面所使用的動詞，為什麼用過去式，是因為它有「與現狀不符」的意思隱含其中。例如，Would you mind if I drove your car? 並非我說開過了你的車子，而是暗指我還沒開過你的車。精確的翻譯是：「假定由我來開你的車，你介意嗎？（If I drove your car, would you mind?）」mind這個字在此屬「不及物動詞」。因此回答的人如果表示同意，卻說出Yes, please go ahead這

樣的話來，那就很搞笑了。正確的回答應該是：No, not at all. 或 No, please. 或 No, go ahead. 或 Of course not. 等等。

如果把mind看作「及物動詞」，那麼就有像Would you mind doing me a favor？這樣的句型。後面的V+ing（doing），長的樣子雖然像現在分詞，但因為它位在mind之後，當作mind的受詞，就性質和作用來看，其實只是「動名詞」（動名詞當然也是名詞的一種囉！）。

假如您遇到障礙或疑難，覺得自己可以搞定，那麼下列這些句子就很實用了：I'll take care of it. I'll see what I can do. I can handle it. Let me try (first). 等等。然而就算自信滿滿，可千萬別拒人於千里之外，用什麼Please leave me alone這樣不近人情且的話喔！

跨文化小叮嚀

身為生物界的一份子，人類雖然貴為萬物之靈，但是同樣具有強烈的「領域感」，其呈現方式經常隨著情境轉換和主客條件的改變，而有所調整。例如：西方文化所強調的個人隱私（狗仔跟拍議題屬之）或身體主權（性騷議題屬之），看似界線模糊，漫無標準，其實取決於情境參與者雙方的默契和共識。假如一方造成了另一方的身／心不悅，即不構成默契和共識。領域不是只有空間領域，還包括延伸領域（如視覺、嗅覺和聲音）和時間領域（如排隊時抽號碼牌，限定時間輪流使用場所等）。

在台北搭捷運，站內公告和車廂內部常會出現一些帶有告誡意味的文宣小品，所規勸的事項，大部份都和尊重他人的「領域感」有關。像是先下後上啦，進入車廂後請往內部移動啦，閱讀書報不要擋到其他乘客啦，後背式背包要側背啦，（講手機等）避免喧嘩啦，搭乘電扶梯時靠右禮讓趕時間的旅客啦（這項是台灣捷運車站的特色，並非放諸四海皆準），不一而足。在歐美國家大眾交通運輸工具場所，則幾乎看不到類似的勸導文宣。

過去搭捷運，最怕「蹺腳客」和「拎傘客」。前者坐在位子上，或高抬二郎腿，將骯髒的鞋底靠在臨座乘客腳邊，令人備感威脅，或伸長飛鴻腿，讓每個經過面前的乘客都得繞道而行；後者總是把傘尖對著別人，前突後插的，既不安全又不衛生。不過，老美尊重「領域感」好像也有點太超過，常聞有住戶因為沒有定期割草，或沒有把曬在屋外的衣服晾整齊，有礙觀瞻，就被鄰居控告。

英文會議屬公共場合，有一定的空間限制和行為規範；若干心照不宣的基本禮儀，仍和尊重彼此的「領域感」有關。以空間領域為例：如果橫排座位只有左右兩個入口，那麼先到的觀眾，應儘量靠中間坐，以方便後到的觀眾就座。以延伸領域為例：如果觀眾（包括講者自己）必須攜帶手機入場，那麼就應該關機，或至少調整為無聲模式；如果菸癮犯了，那麼請移駕到室外，切勿在會場走道或廁所裡抽菸。以時間領域為例：遲到的觀眾不要大喇喇的從台前走過，而應該從後門或側門進來，儘量靠側邊

155

走，輕聲就座；議程排在前面的講者（以及引言人、現場工作人員等）要能掌控時間，切勿欲罷不能，以免佔用到後面議程講者的發言時間。

練習13 （任務目標：分享成果若即若離）

《莊子》書中說有人養了一群猴子，開銷很大，於是想了個妙招。他對著猴群說：「以後每天早上給你們每個吃四顆果子，但是到了黃昏，就只能給你們每個吃三顆果子。」猴兒心想：「怎麼到了晚上少了一顆！」於是激憤不已。主人再道：「這樣好了。以後每天早上給你們每個吃三顆果子，但是到了黃昏，就可以讓你們每個吃四顆果子啦！」猴兒心想：「到了晚上多一顆？Yay！」（表達雀躍，Ya和Yeah均屬誤用）這就是成語「朝三暮四」的由來，可惜後世將它錯解（並接受）為「朝秦暮楚」之意。深層解讀後，這才領會，故事乃暗指我們聽人家講話時，傾向「先入為主」，以此為判斷基礎之餘，往往造成謬誤。

作業想定之一

依照「對事不對人」和「實事求是」的精神，改寫下列英文句子。

【批評別人時】

You did not perform well. (原句) 改寫後…

→You could have performed much better. (不徹底否定對方)

→I think your performance leaves something to be desired. (精確)

→Probably you tried your best, but your performance

fails to prove it. (委婉)

→They delayed their submission of homework. (原句) 改寫後…

→They could have submitted their homework on time. (不徹底否定對方)

→They did not submit their homework on time. (精確)

→If nothing went wrong, they would submit homework on time. (委婉)

There are 3 shortcomings in your presentation. (原句) 改寫後…

→Your presentation could have appeared perfect to me. (不徹底否定對方)

→Your presentation leaves nothing to be desired but 3 things. (精確)

→I will suggest 3 things which you can take into account to improve your presentation. (委婉)

You did not explain it in detail. (原句) 改寫後…

→It should have been explained in detail. (不徹底否定對方)

→Your explanation of it was found short of details. (精確)

→I need your help to give more explanations of it in detail. (委婉)

【讚美自己時】

I am proud of myself. (原句) 改寫後…

→I have a lot of pride. (淡化主觀性)

→Something makes me proud. (歸因於它)

→I don't think I should have much pride, but I am really happy. (委婉)

My idea has never been figured out by anyone else before. (原句) 改寫後…

→The idea I shared had not been proposed by anyone else. (淡化主觀性)

→I wouldn't become the first to figure out the idea if anyone else tried. (歸因於它)

→We all have been working hard, but I am the first who found the idea. How lucky I am! (委婉)

No one else's project is better than mine. (原句) 改寫後…

→No one else did better than what I am doing on this kind of project. (淡化主觀性)

→My project could be the worst if anyone else did the best on his/hers. (歸因於它)

→I feel surprised that other projects leave much more to be desired than mine. (委婉)

Speaking of crisis management, ours is the best team in the world. (原句) 改寫後…

→In these crises, our team came to handle the situation much earlier and acted much better than any other teams involved later. (具體化)

→I haven't seen any other teams that manage a crisis more efficiently and effectively than ours does. (歸因於它)

→If you are looking for a team that could best manage crises, you can count on ours. (委婉)

作業想定之二

　　請認真預備好一份讀書心得書面報告（自己寫的才行，而且要旁徵博引），中、英文不拘），然後根據這份報告，開展成一段長達至少五分鐘左右的英文口頭草稿，其遣詞用字和語氣皆應秉持積極、客觀和中肯的調性，不過份吹捧自己內容的特點，也不過份批評所引證的參考資料弱點。

　　【口頭草稿例文】請參考黑色斜體粗字的部份。

Topic▷ How I Understand Jazz through American Cultures and Vice Versa

　　Jazz is a uniquely American-born musical form with diverse origins. In a sense of cultural exchanges, it has a tendency to influence other music styles outside the U.S. and is also susceptible to them. In general, the pursuit of freedom has become a cultural connotation believed to sufficiently explain what jazz may mean. The proliferation of jazz interpretations in the past 20 years proves very <u>inspirational</u> in the field of jazz studies. For example, ***Robert O'Meally asserts that*** <u>jazz</u> is "not only a music to define, it is a culture"; ***he reminds me of such features as improvisation, time keeping, teamwork, organization***, and so on, which are most frequently found in jazz playing and <u>can be applied to our daily life</u>.

    One of Miles Davis's comments encourages me to develop the topic of my report. He says, "Fewer and fewer black musicians were playing jazz and I could see why, because jazz was becoming <u>the music of the museum</u>". As a jazz musician who went along with the development of American jazz, <u>Davis</u>, because of his pursuit of freedom, in most cases ironically made him an easy target to attack, <u>sometimes</u> <u>considered</u> a musician <u>undermining jazz in the long term</u>.

    An avant-garde jazz trumpeter ***Lester Bowie doubts*** "that <u>the institutionalization of jazz might stifle its creative force</u>". ***Although Bowie's opinion sounds truer if used to interrogate***. . . .[略] Likewise, ***as James Collier mentions***,

jazz can be better interpreted as a cultural mirror, and it is not supposed to arbitrarily belong to any specific ethnic group. *And this is where my argumentation starts.*

Fewer sources have explicitly discussed jazz by way of the American dream. Most of earlier studies focusing on jazz are either more concerned with musicology or unaware of or indifferent to the race issue. The most recent publications have been found more oriented toward cultural studies in terms of globalization. For example, ... [略]

What I am trying to maintain is also what these authors assert. Burton W. Peretti indicates that the progression of jazz styles reflects social changes. . . . [略]

Besides, *many critics and scholars suggest that* American culture is a multi-culturally nurtured by diverse practices, where jazz has played a remarkable role. *I've also learned much from Krin Gabbard.* Tending to see the history of jazz in terms of otherness-oriented points of view, he presents a collection of essays through literature, dance, and visual arts. *This inspires me to propose a notion* of "cultural derivatives" closely related to jazz music.

I feel very much encouraged to develop the notion. It is because a large number of publications have emphasized how much effort jazz musicians in history made to "preserve" themselves and to fulfill their need for self-actualization. *The following authors point out* how market economy influenced a jazz giant. For instance, Scott DeVeaux indicates that the birth and the development of bebop, a popular but revolutionary jazz genre during the 1940s, were inevitably determined by show businesses. *Dan Morgenstern, an expert* on the shows played in jazz concerts, especially *appreciates Louis Armstrong's double role*. In his view, Armstrong was not simply an entertainer but an artist. He played trumpets and sang songs greatly, he was fun onstage, he drew a lot of attention, he earned big fame, and he made money.

However, Gene Lees collects some interviews with leading jazz musicians, showing how racial discrimination has affected their life and work in details. *Francis Davis, who knows a lot about* American culture, jazz genres, and their musicians, *points out* in his most updated studies on jazz *that* the problem of jazz is "its lack of exposure". *My assumption accords with his finding to a certain degree. I also agree with Gary Giddens, who asserts that* the government is not obligated to financially support jazz musicians but provide a guarantee of social mobility. I would say this is what seems indispensable in a democratic country like the U.S. – equal opportunity and free choices. The fans and audiences are just like judges and consumers;

they decide whether people, including jazz musicians, will survive or not. Giddens also indicates that jazz musicians never take publicity for granted; they know it is something to be struggled for.

Of course *the institutionalization of jazz supports my theme*: <u>Where jazz is going</u> and <u>whatever jazz musicians can do</u> for survival are worth it, and this appears irrelevant to self-devaluation among other ethnics. *Let me briefly state my conclusion, which is very similar to Scott DeVeauz's belief* that jazz, despite its feature of blackness, has been moving on the path to institutionalization and thus become <u>more classical</u>. . . . [略]

[濃縮改編自筆者所撰 "A Critical Overview of Jazz Discourse to Be Discussed through the American Dreams," *The Proceedings of 2006 International Conference and Workshop on TEFL & Applied Linguistics* at Ming Chuan University, Taipei: Crane: 2007, pp. 1-8.]

例文<u>雙底線區塊</u>因具多重指涉，或不夠具體（按個別觀眾理解），或需舉例（按個別觀眾需求），極有可能在Q&A階段被觀眾問倒（詳見練習14）。此外，作者引用他人著述或看法時，多半使用中立或積極字眼，透露出自己和大家「所見略同」的意味。在分析的過程中，有需要質疑或辯證之處，也不親上火線，而是讓資料去說明，

「借力使力」，像是第三段落的 [Lester Bowie's doubt] sounds truer if used to interrogate云云。提及到過去相關研究角度的缺漏時，對事不對人，如Fewer sources have explicitly discussed jazz by way of the American dream云云，而且說明原因：Most of earlier studies focusing on jazz are either more concerned with musicology or unaware of or indifferent to the race issue.

THINK TWICE

It is against the instinct deep inside to keep a low profile on how brilliant we are especially when we have achieved something through our toil and intelligence. That is not meant to deny our own effort under all circumstances; rather, it just does no good to behavein a pompous manner if we fail to express ourselves appropriately.

On one hand, when a quote which inspires us a lot is to be introduced to our audience, a tactic often used is to first praise and highlight its advantages and merits. Then we continue to explain the logical tie between the quote and our own idea; more importantly, we will add further

comments like what it means by the differences between the idea of the quote and ours. On the other hand, when a quote or another person's idea is found problematic, one of the safest tactics is not to emphasize how much it leaves to be desired but to stress what could/should/would have been done to better comprehend or improve it.

In most cases, we would humbly propose our viewpoint or approach in terms of similar issues or studies. Ours is surely not perfect; no one else's is, either. Such mental preparedness is believed to help us proceed on the right track.

英語文小叮嚀

　　什麼叫主觀？什麼叫客觀？這兩個詞彙聽起來有些抽象。自己的客觀，往往在別人眼中顯得很主觀，而大家共同的主觀，則往往被認為是某種客觀。愈聽愈玄了吧？比如我想叫小孩乖乖念書，這我自認的客觀，但是小孩可不這麼認為，他會覺得那是你強加在他身上的主觀命令（除非他自己體認到念書的樂趣和諸多好處）。又比如多元社

會有著各種不同政治思想主張的人群，他／她們各自難免覺得自己團體所主張的理念，才是最符合大眾利益的客觀價值，但是有著不同意見的人彼此之間，卻幾乎不可能說服對方，那不就等於一群共同主觀P.K.另一群共同主觀嗎？

英文裡有兩個動詞，用來鑑別何謂客觀、何謂主觀，甚是得力。一個叫describe，另一個叫interpret。前者直譯為「描述」，意指當我們在說明某人某事時，好像照著紋路、線條去描繪那樣，說它是什麼，它應該就是它原來的什麼，容不得我們額外加油添醋；後者直譯為「詮釋」，意指當我們說明某人某事時，彷彿有個什麼想法或價值在背後給我們「下指導棋」，以至於不會說「它是什麼」，而會說「它意味著什麼」。

例如：有職員開會遲到了。主管A說：She arrived at 10 o'clock sharp, but the meeting began at 9:30. I am afraid she might have missed something important here. 主管B說：She is late again because she is always lazy and careless. 哪種回應更接近description呢？沒錯，就是主管A。而主管B明顯是在做一番interpretation，批評有餘，顯實不足。哪一段陳述會讓人感覺比較客觀呢？自然是主管A的說法。

客觀的表達方式有兩個主要特點：一是描述事實，二是根據事實來做推測時，會坦誠說出「我恐怕」、「我覺得」、「我認為」等，以避免武斷。主觀表達的特色則在於，往往用客觀的動詞，搭配看似客觀的因果、條件等，

來包裝主觀的詮釋，或用莫須有的形容詞或其他修飾語來給對象「貼標籤」、「扣帽子」。

跨文化小叮嚀

　　會議英文發表和一般學術出版最大的不同，在於後者為單向傳訊，文詞較犀利、直接，但是一切文責自負，準備皆受讀者的嚴格檢驗；後者用語為雙向交流，文詞較溫和、間接，更像是拋敝磚引珍玉，希望獲得觀眾的誠摯掌聲。這也就是為什麼會議發表活動中，比較少看見針鋒相對場面的緣故，但這並不表示大家參與英文會議都是來和稀泥的。

　　公開分享研究成果，應該是講者最容易得意忘形的時候了。有時講著講著，會不經意流露出「自讚毀他」的味道，在提及或引用前人的學術積累和一家之言時，妄加批評，或是不夠慎重，用了比較強烈的字眼去虧損他人（著作），這樣做都不算得體，也有失厚道。此時反而應該更加冷靜，愈加謙卑，即秉持「不臭屁」原則是也。

　　再說，世俗眼裡，哪有什麼「絕對」的「真理」呢？學術界至今創發的各種典範、理論和觀點，也不過各具特色，各自有相應的套用範圍，哪可能放諸四海皆準呢？因此，講者發表成果，理當用字審慎、中立，不帶感情色彩，留些後路，為將來爭取自我改善的空間，即秉持「不沾鍋」原則是也。

　　講者寧可講自己（成果）的好，也不要講他人（成果）的不好；可以講自己優於他人既有成果之處有哪些，切莫把它講成他人既有成果不如自己之處有哪些；可以說自己有哪些地方能夠再加強，但不必說成自己的東西做的不夠好。親愛的讀友們，諸位掌握了箇中竅門了嗎？

練習14（任務目標：確保結論呼應題旨）

念國小時，某同學出遊，歸來後，在校車上大談美國經。我隨口問：「有科學小飛俠坐的飛機嗎？」他正色道：「當然有囉！有二號大明的座機，也有三號珍珍、四號阿丁、五號阿龍的。」我追問：「一號鐵雄有嗎？」他回：「有啊！我把拔在費城幫我五台都買到了。」我不信：「是玩具吧？」他強調：「是真的飛機，科學小飛俠的！」他叫我星期六去他家樓頂瞧個究竟。時候一到，我手上拿著他抄來的地址，走進一間破舊樓房。大門沒鎖，我向上狂奔，走到最高處。頂樓陽台的門鎖著。我在樓梯間枯坐一上午。同學爽約了。設若講者做報告，下結論，沒呼應題旨，大概就跟放觀眾鴿子差不多吧。

作業想定之一

以下的例子，做為結論，分別具有哪些特點？請（以中文）簡要說明之。

【例一】

The analysis of jazz improvisations that backdrop chosen scenes in "Extinct Pink" deserves further exploration. It reminds us of **a composite of bitter- sweetness in life**. As Mona Hadler points out, "jazz was a combination of improvisation and structure". Structure is built-in. It is the unchangeable. For example, doing the best to look for the

better could be a part of human nature. When responding to such a call, one will get involved in certain competition, if not unavoidable. On the other hand, **improvisation refers not only to crises but to chances**.

The statement as below is to echo what was proposed in my presentation. **Jazz** music by and large **can be seen as discursively synonymous to "hope, strength, optimism, freedom, and creativity"**. The bottom line is that people should reconcile themselves to what life is all about, where bitter-sweetness stimulates **improvisation that requires "playing it by ear" in a flexible or creative way**. Therefore, what this *Pink Panther* episode "Extinct Pink"suggests is more than enjoyment and entertainment. It is, rather, **an approach to a deeper understanding of American Culture**.

[改編自筆者所撰 (結論部份)："There's No Easy Way Out: Black Humor and Black Music," *The Proceedings of 2007 International Conference and Workshop on TEFL & Applied Linguistics at Ming Chuan University*, Taipei: Crane: 2007, pp. 35-39.]

【簡略說明】

　　粗體字的部份為關鍵句，裡面包含了呼應主旨的關鍵詞，在表現手法上，保留兩個最重要的詞彙（如bitter-

sweetness和improvisation）不變，其餘用字則有變化，使意義更加明確和深刻（如refer not only to crises but to chances / discursively synonymous / in a flexible or creative way / an approach / a deeper understanding 等）。首段有節制的引用了他人言論，而後續補充說明的部份，為下一段埋下伏筆。末尾四行除了提醒本文研究範圍，也揭示了日後開展此一研究範圍的可能性，唯講者並未對此多加闡述，亦屬無可厚非。

【例二】

I've found that Ksitigarbha's vows and practice correspond to **the avoidance of misfortune and sorrows** and **the pursuit of ultimate happiness**. This is believed to appear similar to the path to Amitabha's Land of Utmost Bliss and Maitreya's Tusita. Whichever Buddha or/and the "pure land" Mahayana Buddhists are longing for, a **deep awareness of self-autonomy** and an **ultimate liberation from the three-poisons** are quite desirable. In the sutra discussed in my presentation, the two females—the Brahman girl and Radiant Eyes—both Ksitigarbha's former incarnations, are described as heroines with strong filial piety to their moms and with indiscriminate love to all sentient beings suffering, especially those suffering from karmic deeds. What Ksitigarbha has been doing is like a **magic**.

Behind the **magic** is something real: **the better management of life through preventive measures taken to avoid sorrows and pursue happiness**.

[改編自筆者所撰 (結論部份) p. 22, from"The Brahman Girl and Radiant Eyes,"*The Proceedings of 2013 International Conference and Workshop on TEFL & Applied Linguistics* at Ming Chuan University, Taipei: Crane: 2007, pp. 17-24.]

【簡略說明】

　　起始句和結尾句相互呼應之餘，點出了講者欲指陳的中心思想：地藏行願旨在「避苦、趨樂」。第三至六行借用他例（另兩尊佛菩薩的淨土）來說明「自決（覺）與解脫」和地藏菩薩行願的本質相似處。緊接著用最精要的方式回顧了本文研究的重點（《地藏經》裡作為菩薩前身的婆羅門女和光目女），順勢導引出結論當中的核心概念，也是結論破題處方才提過的「避苦、趨樂」，但在表達手法上有些許變化（由名詞轉為動詞，如pursuit of happiness à pursue happiness等）。

【例三】

　　My concluding remark will begin with a reminder of the two hypotheses. First, there is no single and no simple answer to jazz, but **the features, values, and "cultural**

derivatives" of jazz have proven it equivalent to an integral part of American culture**. Second, although there is no definite answer either to the **jazz debates on "black or white"**, when it comes to the creed shared and to the efforts to earn much and avoid failure, such debates may **sound paradoxical and short of profundity**. That's why, as you've seen here, my attempt is to highlight the context that relates between **jazz musicians** and the cultural milieu where the former **play a pivotal role**.

Let me summarize what my analysis has brought about. In history, **Jazz was one of the earliest arenas where African Americans succeeded in drawing much attention**. For many, jazz was taken for granted as a cultural practice labeled as "black", and the label led to confrontations and negotiations. **Confrontations and negotiations occurred at the same time in most cases, and they both gradually extended the jazz discourse and diversified the interpretation of jazz**. Whether financially rich or poor, jazz musicians in general were culturally powerful, and they suggested a tacit understanding of where such a subculture was going. Therefore, **we don't have to side with either color-blindness or narrow-mindedness** when discussing the jazz discourse.

Now I am very close to the end of my presentation.

However, for my research, this is not the end. Actually **I have a plan to continue and elaborate this research**. To fulfill my plan, I will have to explore some more great musicians' lives and performances in jazz, starting from Jelly Roll Morton to Wynton Marsalis, find out what they held in common, and point out what factors made them differ.

If you are interested in this plan, or if you have any suggestion, please let me know. We'll have a lot of ideas to be exchanged in the Q&A session that follows. Welcome to join us. On the slide is my contact information. Thank you for listening.

[濃縮改編自筆者所撰，結論部份："A Critical Overview of Jazz Discourse to Be Discussed through the American Dreams," *The Proceedings of 2006 International Conference and Workshop on TEFL & Applied Linguistics* at Ming Chuan University, Taipei: Crane: 2007, pp. 1-8.]

【簡略說明】

粗體字的部份構成了結論的骨幹。講者於首段重申了本文的假設，提醒觀眾莫落入非黑即白的無謂爭論。次段承接題旨，摻入confrontations與negotiations這兩個關鍵詞彙，透過歷史和社會發展背景，帶出本文最具決定性的一句話：「爵士論述因而逐步得到擴充／延伸；針對爵士音樂場域所做的文化詮釋亦變得多元」。於是結尾又加強

道：為求客觀，「探討爵士論述無須落入兩端。」結論甫畢，講者另針對未來（對自己研究相關議題）的展望略作說明，但並未過度解釋細節，因此不至於顯得頭重腳輕。

作業想定之二

利用練習13的作業想定之二，以自己的讀書心得報告（並非本書的心得範例）為基礎，自我檢視一番，用中文，簡要說明您的結論具有哪些特點。

【結論檢視】

〈「結論」可謄寫或縮小列印浮貼在此〉

【簡略說明】

THINK TWICE

A conference presenter calls and responds by himself/herself. Sometimes the role he/she plays is similar to that played by a ventriloquist. What makes a presenter and a ventriloquist different is that the former is required to argue for and explain what has been promised while the latter will not have to do so.

A frequently found problem is that presenters could help result In a lot of findings without substantially answering to the questions proposed in the beginning. Another problem is that the results may not exactly correspond to the hypothesis or purpose given. In the former case, if the presenters are not ready to answer a question raised, they should have either dropped it or revised it. In the latter case, if the results, unfortunately, end up incongruous with the presenters' assumption or intention, they should have acknowledged that there is certain discrepancy found and explained why it happens and how they could have otherwise done to avoid it or get

improved.

Honesty is the best policy. The audience do not ask for more. They attend the conference presentation and look more forward to ways to approach possible solutions to a problem than to the promised answers.

說到英語行文習慣，筆者總結爲兩句話。一是口說不怕囉嗦，能讓聽者易懂就好，二是手寫不妨直接，能讓讀者省力才對。例如，寫作文，下結論，如果我們狂用過去學過的一堆連接語，像in all, in short, in conclusion, to sum up, last but not least什麼的，說實在，並不容易討老外讀者的喜，不只因爲它們看起來既便宜又老套，更因爲它們是「可被取代的」累贅。那麼如果用在口頭表達呢？想必無可厚吧？可偏偏它們依舊不容易討好觀眾，原因是：它們並非不夠囉嗦，而是它們的囉嗦，無法爲聽者帶來意趣（意義＋趣味）。

每當講者說in all的時候，大家心裡可能OS（off-screen）道：「終於要解脫了。」講者說in short，聽者可能OS：「原來前面這般冗長。」講者說in conclusion，聽者會OS：「要不然咧？」講者說To sum up，聽者就OS：「我討

178

厭數學」講者說last but not least，聽者便OS：「二十一世紀了，有人這樣說話的嗎？」這種事情的「眉角」在於，觀眾並不奢望創意，但是很在意講者是否有求新求變的誠意。

　　我們不期待每個人上台都變成滔滔不絕的演說家，但是爲觀眾換個說法，總還可以試著做做看吧？例如：試著把剛剛提到的那些結尾連接語，開展成一個帶有「主詞＋動詞」結構的簡單句型，不至於太難吧？例如：in all → all I have said → take a look at all I have said → Let me take a look at all I have said briefly；或者像in conclusion → my conclusion → My conclusion is that . . .；或者像last but not least →（素人版）This is the last part, but it is also something important [which we should not ignore]. 或（升級版）It's time to end my presentation, but I'd like to share some more, which I think we cannot afford to ignore.

跨文化小叮嚀

　　無論書面陳述，還是口頭發表，訂定結論的時候，要幫讀者或觀眾把「糖果包裝」打開。此時不要再別人去猜我們的心思，而應該利用最簡潔的表達方式，爲通篇內容下個最終的，也是最大的註腳。它可以舊事重提，但不能狂炒冷飯；它可以重申要旨，但不應了無新意。結論內容假使給人聽起來的感覺像「跳針」，遍尋無「梗」，那就

沒有下的必要了。

　　結論如果切題，未嘗不能旁徵博引，但不宜繼續摻入過多分析，也不宜針對本題前述未竟之處多做補充。前面遺漏，現在雄雄想起之處，寧可放在問答時段（Q&A session）追加補充，也不要讓它跑來跟結論「搶生意」。下「結論」，好比戰鬥結束後，需要步兵「清理戰場」那樣，其目的不在重啟戰端，而在確保戰果，並判斷是否需要就地整補，抑或繼續追剿敵軍。

　　清理戰場是筆者形容結論所用的隱喻。就地整補，指的是今後不再延伸或開展相關議題，通常代表自己的研究努力已經告一段落，但會後仍需不斷刪修或增補，使成果更臻完善；繼續追剿，指的是研究成果或進展顯然有意猶未盡之處，因此向觀眾或讀者宣告並解釋自己未來打算延伸探討的方向為何。

　　在結論裡，也有人喜歡加入所謂的「展望」。不過，許多講者卻片面將它錯會為對客觀現象趨勢的期待和建議，因此表達的時候，只就相關議題或政策方向提出意見和臆測，甚至用它來取代結論。但嚴格來說，「展望」應該主要還是用來說明對自己研究主題、範圍、方法等等的展望；更重要的是，它並不等同於結論。

練習15（任務目標：掌握問答接招技巧）

　　過去參加棒球校隊時，承蒙李來發先生指導揮棒動作：打外角球，揮棒別向外硬撈，而是要縮棒，微微側身，用打內角的感覺輕推即可。後來用在大專盃，果真有效，擊出一支反方向二壘安打。有次跟友校比賽，在首次打席中，因惦記著學長告誡「不可由下往上撈球」，揮棒時有些遲疑，最後被大幅度曲球三振；第二次上場打擊，便不再乖乖聽話，面臨對方一模一樣的大幅度曲球，毫不遲疑，完全用撈的，揮出生平打過最遠的球，用我年輕時的快腿，跑回一支場內全壘打。在會議Q&A階段，頗像投打對決，態度上不宜「吾道一以貫之」，技巧上也沒有什麼「球來就打」這回事。總的來說，就是看人說話，見招拆招。

作業想定

　　以練習13作業想定二的例文為藍本，站在講者立場，針對下列觀眾四種發問類型，草擬英文口頭應答講稿。

【一箭雙鵰型】

　　問者：*Would you explain why you said that the interpretations of jazz in the past 2 decades are very inspirational in the studies of jazz? Second, is there any reason and phenomenon that makes you feel that jazz music has become more classical. I remember jazz was once a national pop music in the U.S. during the 1930s, and many of to-*

day's jazz music are supported by elements from other music forms like rock'n'roll, hip-hop, etc. What do you think?

答者：Let me start with the second question. I didn't say jazz sounds more like classical music. I tend to define "classical" as something that has been developed and refined to a very high degree, not necessarily whatever similar to European classical music. In that sense, jazz has become American classical music. I agree, as you said, and also as I mentioned in my presentation, today's jazz may not sound so "pure" as before. But that's the way it is: jazz accepts reforms. It never dies; it has just been transformed into something else. Even European classical music changes, right? The standards won't change much, but that does not hinder their exchanges and transformations with other music forms. So, I don't think I can give any direct answer to this question. All I can do is to make clear how [停頓半秒] many others and I have looked at jazz. Well, pardon me, what is your first question?

　　此類型問話，可能多達兩個（含）以上的問題。如果時間有限，以及為了公平起見，更為了避免破壞發問次數的「行情」，通常如果問到第三個問題，講者就要考慮委婉勸阻對方繼續發問了。

　　面對同一人提兩則問題，講者應先從第二個問題答

起。這樣做，好處在於，第二個問題因為是最後提的，所以令人印象深刻，可以好整以暇的回答。答完後，如果忘記第一個問題，可以很大方的，理所當然的（**OS:**誰叫你要一口氣問兩個問題，誰記得了那麼多？）請對方重說一次問題。（再**OS:**如果連你自己或其他觀眾都忘了，我就不能，也不必答了）。

【借題發揮型】

〈甲型〉

問者：*I think jazz is not really a jazz form. It sounds like a mixture of many different things. So, what is jazz? The question itself is very hard to define, and the possible answers to it we've already heard are probably more confusing. For me, I don't see anything profound in the history of jazz. It's just like a process where musicians play bizarre tunes and thus attract certain fans. You know, the process is pretty much like those concerning other music forms. It's a business, having not much to do with the so-called "culture". If the government agrees to financially support it, that'll be fine. But it could violate the mechanism of free market and democracy. If jazz musicians....*

答者：Excuse me, what is the question anyway?

〈乙型〉

問者：*I read the book you mentioned, the one commented by Miles Davis. I cannot agree with his idea more that jazz has become "the music of museum". Many jazz critics mentioned that too. You know sometimes I was wondering why Davis used the term "museum" to describe jazz. He had the final say. I would say in some sense he created and developed jazz, but he also made it fall into the abyss somehow. Louis Armstrong is the other type. He....*

答者：Excuse me. I don't think I got the point. Would you clarify the question? Make it short, please.

　　甲型問話，一講沒完沒了，而且內容和講者所提論點很少有交集，純然抒發聽者個人己見，邏輯也有點「跳痛」。判別這類問話的訣竅是，如果對方壓根兒沒用到以任何wh-（所謂6Ws: where, when, how, who, what, why）起首的句型，這時講者就開始要有警覺了，要委婉暗示對方：你是在問問題？決不能讓「提問者」繼續海侃下去，否則會耽誤到別人提問的時間。

　　乙型問話，同樣喋喋不休，差別在於，一開始有提到講者所借用的關鍵詞彙。本來應該就此打住的，看是要問the music of museum代表什麼深義，還是要問它對於jazz的文化論述造成多大影響；未料提問人沒有罷休的意思，竟開始自作回答，講沒多久，好像又不是在自作

回答，話題不知偏到哪裡去了。由於乙型問話「尚屬有救」，因此講者給了對方一次重申問題的機會。

【尋求認同型】

問者：*You quoted that jazz as a cultural connotation could be found at many places in our daily life. The examples you mentioned include improvisation and many other... Sorry I don't remember the rest. I'd like to emphasize improvisation. Does that mean people's willingness to accept uncertainty and mental preparation for possible changes or ordeals? In other words, does that mean people's ability to remain flexible in a situation where solutions are desperately needed and compromise is highly suggested for survival. What's your opinion about it? How would you interpret improvisation?*

答者：The two questions are relevant to the topic, and they appear familiar with each other. So, I'd like to answer both at the same time; I hope you won't mind. [其實沒有打算要回答第一個問題] First, we all agree that improvisation is a term primarily used in music. Its most frequently used synonym is spontaneity, which has been widely used in literature. Inspired by the compositions of jazz and the way how jazz music is played, I have a similar idea shared by many jazz critics that the word improvisation, or whatever

else you'd like to rename it, spontaneity, for instance, is supposed to mean positive qualities like negotiations, freedom, anti-slavery, human capacities, etc. I know this may sound like a metaphor, but I cannot help but let you know that when watching a jazz band playing music onstage, on the spot I see these musicians as some kinds of liberators, whose name is "unbound Prometheus". Second, ... [略]

　　提問者並未直截了當說出問題，而是在簡短發表意見之後，設下一個陷阱（雖然不是故意的，但是動機不見得純潔），要講者提個意見。但是由於會議英文場合並非辯論大會，講者無論如何必須盡最大努力與觀眾／聽者保持和諧。當然，西方人一向習慣當面問對和批評，似乎沒什麼大不了的，而且講者願意按提問人要求，給個兩句批評，自然無可厚非，可是這樣做的話，意義大不大，恐怕還得三思。

　　如果講者回應的是批評，那等於給人下不了台（除非發問人可以抗辯，但這並非Q&A階段該做的事）。如果講者回應的是嘉許，那等於在極短的判斷時間之內為對方加持或背書，如果正確倒好，皆大歡喜，對方也滿足了虛榮，萬一有點閃失，講者的專業形象則多少會受到波及。與其這樣那樣，不如直接切入「真正的問題」，也就是最後問的那段how would you interpret improvisation? 講者直搗黃龍的結果，等於間接回應了對方第一個「不是問

題」的問題，既不傷己，更不損人；最重要的是：它緊扣講者presentation本身的內容！

【虛擬情境型】

〈甲例〉

問者：*As a jazz fan, I am especially interested in the part where you mentioned that the problem of jazz is its lack of exposure. It could be true. What if the problem were solved? Does that mean getting jazz institutionalized would become no longer necessary or worthwhile?*

答者：I am a jazz fan too. We both know well that jazz has always been produced, played, and appreciated by a small group of people. The problem is [停頓半秒] this is not exactly a problem. This is what happens. Unless we figure out how to attract more people to get involved in the jazz industry, it will be impractical, I'm afraid, to say anything about an imagined situation like that. But I thank you for the question anyway. One thing I'd like to remind you here is that I didn't mean to emphasize how much [停頓半秒] jazz practitioners would benefit from institutionalization. More students attending schools and graduated as jazz musicians do not guarantee the popularity and prosperity of jazz. You know jazz was not supposed to be created and developed that way.

〈乙例〉

問者：*In the U.S., if there were no institutionalization of jazz, what would American culture look right now? And what could it mean to the jazz industry?*

答者：I find it hard to assume that this could happen. **If** jazz had its endless momentum from the grass-roots, there were probably no need to institutionalize it. **When** it has been developed and refined to an enormously high degree with the fact that there is a smaller audience involved, then such momentum will not be simply supported by the grass-roots. There are also two things we need to take into account very seriously. First, **is it likely that** in the near future the population of jazz fans and musicians is getting as big as that of pop music? Even so, will such population growth be kept steady? Second, **do most of us really accept that** jazz is a symbol of American Culture? Is it worthwhile to facilitate the institutionalization of jazz? Maybe we need to think twice, and **hopefully something would come up to refer to the questions raised on you assumption**.

假設性的問題不容易回答，不只因為它缺乏可靠的條件或佐證，更因為它看似緊扣主題論點，其實多半無關宏旨。如果問的不得法，何異於「腦筋急轉彎」耍kuso？

既然怎麼回答都不易討好，動輒得咎，講者面對這種「虛問」，大可不必「實答」；犯不著為此砸了自己的招牌。真要卯起來答，那就用「刀切豆腐兩面光」來回覆發問者。此時講者需要再度負起「拉回主題」的重責大任，不能因為這類問題好像能夠引發觀眾的興趣就跟著「撩落去」。

首先，若作「虛答」，講者可向提問人解釋道，對方所提情況目前並不存在，若要探討這類問題，是否應先針對可能造成這類情境的變數，包括外部環境和內部因素，做一番深入淺出討論，唯受限於時間和主題範圍，目前並不適合在此多做申論。其次，若欲用「刀切豆腐兩面光」的方式來答覆，那麼應儘量運用條件子句（假設語氣），比如說若A則P，若B則Q，但是我們無法確定是否A或B會發生。換言之，觀眾「假如」來，講者就「假如」去。

THINK TWICE

The Q&A session is assumed to be the last chance by which the presenter and the audience exchange ideas. If lucky enough, afterthe conference, a presenter may earn intangible credit from or long-term friendship with his/her audience. But that seems rare to most conference presenters when they are still young and inexpe-

rienced.

Some may argue that the audience should be allowed to meet their need in a presentation, such as giving a concluding remark or an oratorical statement on the presented stuff. Because the time given is always limited, and since the leading role in a conference presentation is the presenter, who deserves more time and space in the Q&A session, it will sound impractical to welcome whoever is not charged to usurp the discursive power that is supposed to be mostly-wielded by the presenter.

In that sense, therefore, when questioned or challenged, a conference presenter acts more like a defender, whose *power* has not much to do with authority but the right to justify.

英語文小叮嚀

店家怕遇到奧客，那麼在英文會議的場子要是碰上了總在challenge我們的奧客怎麼辦？筆者並非以小人心度君子腹，實在是，中西皆然，在會議問答時段，總會有人表

面上像在問問題，其實根本說個沒完，形同抒發己見；要不然就淨問一些與主題無關的東西，牽扯太遠。但是遇到那些問到我們痛處，問到我們習而不察的，那就絕非等閒之輩，而是救命的行家！

好了，要是果真遇上奧客怎麼辦？這類事情，用愈簡單明瞭的方式去化解，愈好，愈有效。遇上喋喋不休者，講者可直接打斷，說：Excuse me, what is your question exactly? 或者 Excuse me, would you please make the question short? 有的講者會說What's the point? 可是那樣太直接，語氣顯的不耐，筆者並不建議使用。

遇提問不合胃口，或問問題不按牌理出牌者，講者或可說The question sounds interesting, but I am not sure if I can answer it right now. 或可說Well, what do you think? 對方若窮追猛打，講者在不損及自己專業的前提下，可以考慮「丟一塊糖」讓人充充饑，聊勝於無，說道：I am not in a position to comment on that, but if you insist, my two cents are.... （我恐怕不適合對此發表評論，但如果閣下堅持的話，我倒可以表示一點淺見，詳情如下…）。

假使遇上行家，讓人一時答不上來，講者可說：I don't think I've ever thought about that; would you mind sharing some suggestions? 或者說：I am afraid it will be irresponsible of me to give any answers to the question before doing more homework. 除非講者十分確定雙方實力差距頗大（例

如教授和學生間，或內行人和門外漢間），沒有專業性被質疑的餘地，否則不宜用像You got me.（你問倒我了）這類美式幽默來示弱或表達善意。

跨文化小叮嚀

　　筆者最後不揣淺陋，針對會議結尾的問答階段，分享幾種可供講者參考的戰術。一是「會前佈線」法，多見於出版推廣或學術研討。消極面，意在避免冷場，牽制奧客；積極面，意在主導話題，拋磚引玉。講的更白一點：有的場子，問的人和答的人，契合度之高，彷彿前者做球給後者殺。

　　其次是「雨露均霑」法，適用於各類會議，尤其觀眾人數較多的場子，意在避免重複點選同一區位的觀眾（無論發問是否踴躍），用以活絡場面，平衡觀點。第三是「夫子自道」法，尤其當觀眾反應冷淡，無人提問時，講者可利用機會彌補疏漏，同時自問自答，進能拋磚引玉，退可填補時間。第四是「借題發揮」法，當觀眾發問太少，現場遺留空檔太多，除了夫子自道之外，仍可透過已經答過的問題，加以補充說明或延伸討論。

　　另一方面，觀眾提的問題再怎麼瞎，再怎麼扯，講者都不應該拒絕回應，但是可以選擇性、重點式的答覆。切忌當面批評觀眾，說什麼你這個問題不對，那個問題不好；這樣一來，會顯得講者器量小，風度差，枉費方才發

表過程當中的付出。

　　如果有的問題實在無解，或者無須答覆，講者亦應耐性解釋不予作答的原因，用詞儘量委婉、懇切，給人留點尊嚴（台諺云：也「給自己留一點讓別人打聽。」）任何一位講者，任憑他專業強，本事高，如果個性剛，態度狂，再逆來順受的觀眾，也不會打從心裡服他的氣。但也不必心虛氣短，姿態委屈，言語過謙，以免讓多數腦筋不擅拐彎的「直腸子」老外誤以為講者真的沒本事，甚至因此引發不可測的，來自觀眾的尖銳批評。

挑戰會議英文情境

－與朋友、同事或同學搭檔，完成以下15道測試。

　　請自選話題，將它開展成一份英文口頭報告，但是您的搭檔只有三分鐘的時間聽您發表。發表結束後，請您的搭檔寫下心得，看看是否有提到您的發表動機、方法或流程，以及成果或結論。然後和搭檔互換角色，重新演練此活動。

Worksheet 1-1 (making plans, sharing ideas, and putting them down in the box)

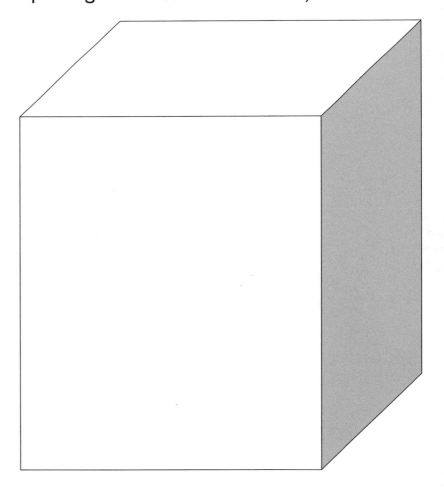

Worksheet 1-2 (teamwork results)

挑戰02（不著痕跡誘發共鳴）

　　請自選話題，將它開展成一份英文口頭報告。然後以這份報告為基礎，發表一段簡短的開場白。結束後，請您的搭檔（虛擬觀眾）回饋意見，講講（或寫寫）您的開場白是否有故事性、普遍性和切身性。然後互換角色，重新演練。

Worksheet 2-1 (making plans, sharing ideas, and putting them down in the box)

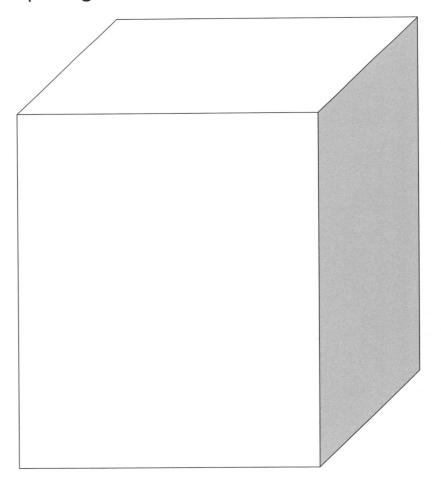

Worksheet 2-2 (teamwork results)

挑戰03（掌握措詞力道輕重）

　　請自選時事話題，開展成兩份長度各約三到五分鐘的英文口頭報告。版本一的口吻（語氣）和用字可以強硬或尖銳些，版本二則要圓緩、委婉和中立一些。發表結束後，請您的搭檔（虛擬觀眾）回饋感想。然後互換角色，重新演練。

Worksheet 3-1 (making plans, sharing ideas, and putting them down in the box)

Worksheet 3-2 (teamwork results)

挑戰04（理順發音咬字難處）

　　從英文報章雜誌中任選（生活化主題較好）一篇短文，不必理解通篇大意，但要查明所有單字的正確發音。接下來，請您根據本書練習4學到的訣竅，朗誦該篇短文。唸完後，請您的搭檔提出指正或讚美。然後互換角色，重新演練。

Worksheet 4-1 (making plans, sharing ideas, and putting them down in the box)

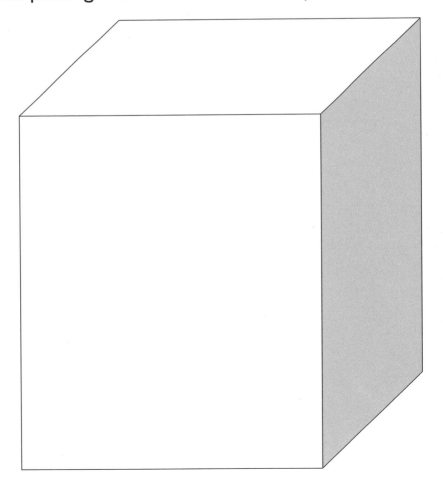

Worksheet 4-2 (teamwork results)

挑戰05（揣摩簡報備忘竅門）

　　請自選話題，在您的搭檔面前，做個長度約五分鐘的英文口頭報告，全程須播放PPT投影。投影片製作以精簡為要，內容儘量以單字或片語來呈現，且至少運用本書練習5當中的兩種方法。然後互換角色，重新演練，並寫下心得。

Worksheet 5-1 (making plans, sharing ideas, and putting them down in the box)

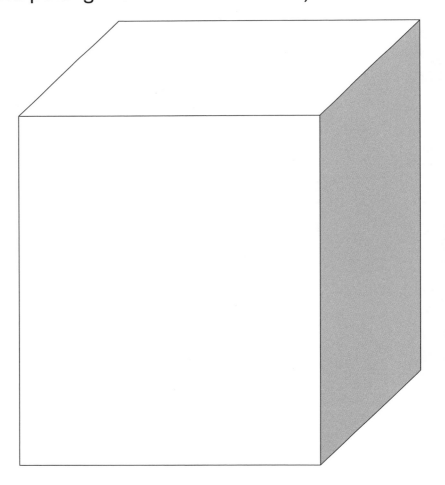

Worksheet 5-2 (teamwork results)

挑戰06（控制口語速度節拍）

　　從英文報章雜誌中任選一篇社論，不必理解通篇大意，但要查明所有單字的正確發音。接下來，請您根據本書練習6學到的訣竅，朗誦該篇文章。唸完後，請您的搭檔提出指正或讚美。然後互換角色，重新演練，並寫下心得。

Worksheet 6-1 (making plans, sharing ideas, and putting them down in the box)

Worksheet 6-2 (teamwork results)

　　請自選話題，在您的搭檔面前，做個長度約五分鐘的英文口頭報告，全程須播放PPT投影。口頭發表時，試著根據練習7的節奏（投影片1,3,5,7與2,4,6,8輕重有別）來執行。結束後，互換角色，重新演練，並寫下心得。

Worksheet 7-1 (making plans, sharing ideas, and putting them down in the box)

Worksheet 7-2 (teamwork results)

挑戰08（利用圖表畫龍點睛）

從英文報章雜誌中任選一篇文章，查明關鍵詞彙的定義與發音，理解文意，把通篇的關鍵概念或數據轉成圖表（種類不拘，請自行決定），透過PPT呈現出來，並以英文口語說明之。做完後，請和您的搭檔互換角色，重新演練。

Worksheet 8-1 (making plans, sharing ideas, and putting them down in the box)

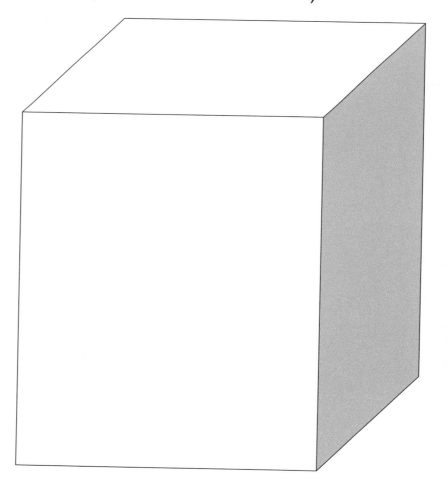

Worksheet 8-2 (teamwork results)

挑戰09（解釋數據言簡意賅）

　　從英文報章雜誌中任選一篇涉及數據統計的文章，查明關鍵詞彙的定義與發音，理解文意，製作（並播放）PPT，以口頭解釋內容給您的搭檔聽，過程中必須運用「取譬法」、「換詞法」和「指義法」其中至少兩種方法。做完後，請和您的搭檔互換角色，重新演練，並寫下心得。

Worksheet 9-1 (making plans, sharing ideas, and putting them down in the box)

Worksheet 9-2 (teamwork results)

挑戰10（拿捏影片撥放時機）

　　請從YouTube等相關網站，任選並觀賞一段長度至少半小時以上的英文紀錄片。然後據此寫下心得，發表一份長達五分鐘的英文口頭報告，過程中只能插播一次（該片）影視片段，並按本書練習9的原則提供必要說明。做完後，請和您的搭檔交換角色，重新演練。最後，請相互批評，並寫下心得。

Worksheet 10-1 (making plans, sharing ideas, and putting them down in the box)

Worksheet 10-2 (teamwork results)

挑戰11（使令觀眾回心轉意）

　　請從網上（TED或YouTube等）尋找免費分享演講的影片，任選一段（長度以不超過20分鐘為宜）口頭簡報或會議演說，至少觀賞兩次，根據本書練習11提供的原則和技巧，與您的搭檔分別寫下心得，提出影片講者的優點與缺失。寫好後，請您和您的搭檔互相分享所寫下的心得內容，並進行比較和討論。

Worksheet 11-1 (making plans, sharing ideas, and putting them down in the box)

Worksheet 11-2 (teamwork results)

挑戰12（處理危機由剝而復）

　　假設您花了三天，盡心盡力設計了一份精美而詳實的PPT，結果到了英文會議現場，臨到發表時才發現PPT檔案存錯了，既沒在電子郵件裡，也沒在隨身碟中，手頭上更沒有備忘卡片。很不巧，緊張和急迫之下，頭腦竟然一片空白。請您（中、英不拘）臨機應變，提出解決方案，化解此一窘境，以順利完成發表。做完想定後，請您和您的搭檔互換角色，重新演練，並寫下心得。

Worksheet 12-1 (making plans, sharing ideas, and putting them down in the box)

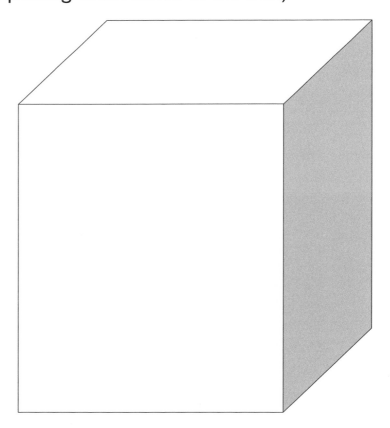

Worksheet 12-2 (teamwork results)

挑戰13（分享成果若即若離）

　　請任選一部文學或影視作品，閱讀或觀賞完畢後，在您的搭檔面前，發表一份三分鐘左右的口頭書評或影評。發表過程中，必須留意語氣是否中肯、委婉，對事不對人。做完後，請和您的搭檔互換角色，重新演練，並寫下心得。

Worksheet 13-1 (making plans, sharing ideas, and putting them down in the box)

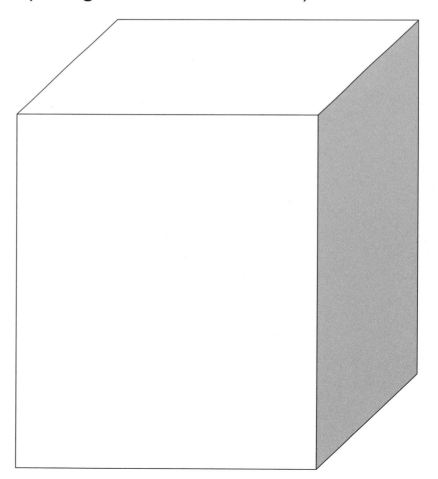

Worksheet 13-2 (teamwork results)

挑戰14（確保結論呼應題旨）

　　請任選一部文學或影視作品，閱讀或觀賞完畢後，在您的搭檔面前，發表一份五分鐘左右的口頭書評或影評。發表結束前必須注意：您的結論是否能夠用稍具創意的說法來呼應主旨。過後，請和搭檔互換角色，重新演練，寫下心得。

Worksheet 14-1 (making plans, sharing ideas, and putting them down in the box)

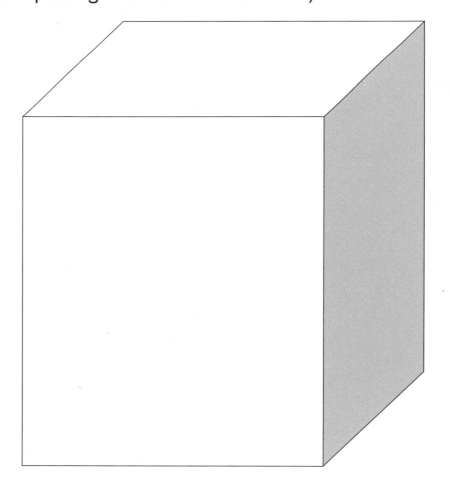

Worksheet 14-2 (teamwork results)

挑戰15（掌握問答接招技巧）

　　在〔挑戰14〕的基礎上，追加一段Q & A的議程，過程中請您扮演發問的「奧客」，同時讓您的搭檔扮演講者來應答。做完後，請和搭檔互換角色，重新演練，來回數次，並寫下心得。

Worksheet 15-1 (making plans, sharing ideas, and putting them down in the box)

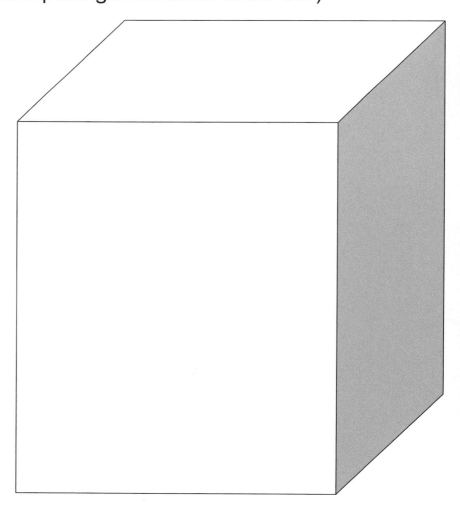

Worksheet 15-2 (teamwork results)

_____

_____

_____

_____

_____

_____

_____

_____

_____

_____

_____

_____

_____

國家圖書館出版品預行編目資料

全面搞定會議英文／張其羽著.
— 初版. — 臺北市：五南，2015.06
　　　面；　　公分.
ISBN 978-957-11-8115-8（平裝）

1.英語　2.會議　3.會話

805.188　　　　　　　　　　104007373

1XOC

全面搞定會議英文

作　　者 — 張其羽

發 行 人 — 楊榮川

總 編 輯 — 王翠華

主　　編 — 朱曉蘋

封面設計 — 劉好音

出 版 者 — 五南圖書出版股份有限公司

地　　址：106台北市大安區和平東路二段339號4樓

電　　話：(02)2705-5066　　傳　　真：(02)2706-6100

網　　址：http://www.wunan.com.tw

電子郵件：wunan@wunan.com.tw

劃撥帳號：01068953

戶　　名：五南圖書出版股份有限公司

台中市駐區辦公室/台中市中區中山路6號

電　　話：(04)2223-0891　　傳　　真：(04)2223-3549

高雄市駐區辦公室/高雄市新興區中山一路290號

電　　話：(07)2358-702　　傳　　真：(07)2350-236

法律顧問　林勝安律師事務所　林勝安律師

出版日期　2015年6月初版一刷

定　　價　新臺幣300元